Goodbye to
Atlantis
Troon Harrison

Goodbye to
Atlantis

Troon Harrison

Stoddart Kids
TORONTO · NEW YORK

Published in Canada in 2001 by
Stoddart Kids, a division of
Stoddart Publishing Co. Limited
895 Don Mills Road, 400-2 Park Centre, Toronto, Ontario M3C 1W3

Published in the United States in 2002 by
Stoddart Kids, a division of
Stoddart Publishing Co. Limited
PMB 128, 4500 Witmer Estates, Niagara Falls, New York 14305-1386

www.stoddartkids.com

To order Stoddart books please contact General Distribution Services
In Canada Tel. (416) 213-1919 Fax (416) 213-1917
Email cservice@genpub.com
In the United States Toll-free tel. 1-800-805-1083 Toll-free fax 1-800-481-6207
Email gdsinc@genpub.com

05 04 03 02 01   1 2 3 4 5

National Library of Canada Cataloguing in Publication Data

Harrison, Troon, 1958–
Goodbye to Atlantis

ISBN 0-7737-6229-9

I. Title.

PS8565.A6587G66   2001   jC813'.54   C2001-902294-8
PZ7.H25616Go   2001

Cover design: Carol Francisco / Francisco Creative Images
Text design and typesetting: Kinetics Design & Illustration
Photo of horse and wave: www.comstock.com
Photo of girl: Corbis Images   Photo of boy: Eyewire, Inc.

THE CANADA COUNCIL | LE CONSEIL DES ARTS
FOR THE ARTS | DU CANADA
SINCE 1957 | DEPUIS 1957

We acknowledge for their financial support of our publishing program the Canada Council, the Ontario Arts Council, and the Government of Canada through the Book Publishing Industry Development Program (BPIDP).

Printed and bound in Canada

*In memory of my grandmothers
on both sides of the Atlantic:
Alice MacCallum and Florence Nicholas.*

ACKNOWLEDGMENTS

With thanks to Angela Broome, librarian at the Courtney Library in Truro, Cornwall, for research into the Atlantis myth; to the Coast Guard in Falmouth for explaining their work; to Kathryn Cole, a sensitive and considerate publisher; to Carol Francisco for enthusiastically contributing her design expertise; to the National Seal Sanctuary in Gweek for sharing their rescued orphans; and to Heather, Ross, and Thomas for accompanying me on the cliffs.

As always, with love and thanks to Chris and Ripley who searched for shells and adjectives on the beaches of St. Ives.

PROLOGUE

Math With My Mother

My mother is ten
toenails painted like seashells,
two legs smooth as glossy paper,
her 28 teeth perfectly aligned, white
as chalk. My mother is a thousand
smiles in front of camera lenses
that click open and shut
like mouths swallowing her
whole — but my mother's two lips
keep smiling and never speak.
My mother has no words
for me: no, none, nada, nothing.
Is zero the place to start counting
or the place where everything ends?

Stella MacLeod, May 2001

CHAPTER ONE

There's something you need to know about me and it's this: I have two different kinds of days in my life. First, there are the days when I feel normal, just plain old me — Stella MacLeod with hair hanging down any way it chooses and hay on my T-shirt. On those kind of days, I don't feel much older than I did in grade two. But on the other kind of days, I know it's time to start being Seriously Mature. On these days, it takes me an hour in the bathroom to get presentable for school or, if it's a weekend, I spend ages in my room with my best friend, Ashley, studying the glossy pages of *Seventeen* magazine and discarding most of the clothes in my closet as unsuitable.

When I woke up on the morning of my fourteenth birthday, I knew right away it was a day to be Seriously Mature. Barefoot, I padded across the warped pine floor to my open window.

"Malibu!" I called, and let out a piercing whistle. My horse's mahogany-colored ears swiveled toward the sound. His white blaze shone in the early morning sun, and dew sparkled in the pasture. The air smelled of sweetness — ripening corn, hollyhock flowers — and already the maple trees seemed limp and thick with heat. A perfect July day, I thought with satisfaction. In fact, most of the day turned out great; it was only toward evening that things began falling apart.

The first thing I wanted to decide on this birthday morning was what to do about my hair. I'd dyed it blonde the previous fall, but that had mostly all grown out and now my hair was back to its usual color, halfway between golden and red (a sort of onion-skin color). I decided that today I'd crimp it; something I hadn't tried before. It took forever, using the crimping iron I'd borrowed from Ashley. Once my hair was taken care of, I applied fluorescent orange polish to my nails while the rest of the house began to wake up. Of course, you couldn't tell in the bright morning light that the polish was fluorescent; I just had to take the label's word for it. But I liked the idea that I would glow in the dark — the knowledge made me feel differently about myself, as though there was more to me than met the eye.

My father's low voice muttered something on the stairs, and then my twin brother's feet clumped noisily on the wooden treads. It's impossible to move quietly in a one-hundred-year-old farmhouse, so I always know when members of my family are around.

Once the polish was dry, I rummaged through my closet and hauled out a sundress. Too babyish, I thought, regarding myself in the mirror. All those little ruffles on the bodice reminded me of kindergarten. Finally I settled for a pair of black leggings and a baggy, black silk shirt embroidered with a dragon in silver thread. I'd found it at a secondhand store; Ashley said it was retro but I liked it because I could imagine my mother wearing something like it. The silk floated against me; I felt mature and glamorous and like someone else.

I thumped downstairs and into the big kitchen where all the faces in my family turned toward me. My dad pulled me into a hug against his soft cotton shirt and for one moment I relaxed against him because he really is a great dad, even though he nags me about doing homework instead of reading fashion magazines.

"Heya," said Noah, hugging me with only one arm because of the basketball held in the other. He gave me a friendly grin, his freckles creasing up on his nose and his onion-skin hair sticking out on one side of his head.

Pearl bustled over from the stove with plates of pancakes in both hands. She set them on the long wooden table before hugging me. "Look at you, so grown-up," she said. "I don't know where the time has gone."

Which was a funny thing to say when you think about it, because Pearl should know if anyone does. I mean, she's been housekeeping for Dad, and feeding Noah and me, for the last eight years. And then, before that, she babysat us whenever my mom needed time to herself.

"Real maple syrup!" said Noah greedily, and Pearl said, "Sit down and eat those pancakes while they're hot. You can have your presents afterward."

Trust Pearl to be bossing us around even on our birthday, but actually I was glad for an excuse to pull out a wooden chair and plop quickly into it. The last thing I wanted to do was hug Skye, who's been my dad's weird girlfriend for the last ten months. Hovering two feet away from my chair, she was waiting for a chance to be friendly. She must have driven out from town early, from the apartment she lives in above her art gallery. I forked a pancake and reached for the butter.

"Happy birthday, both of you," Skye said with a smile, realizing she wasn't going to get close to me. Noah — who doesn't seem to mind her being around — said "thanks" and stuck his elbow into my ribs. I gulped a mouthful of Pearl's melting, fluffy pancake and said "thanks," too. I also saw the look that passed between Dad and Skye: that tentative, hopeful smile she uses around me; that kind, encouraging nod from him. Too kind, that's the problem with my dad. Why else would he put up with Skye's weirdness?

I glanced at her over my steaming plate, checking her out as she poured green tea for herself and Dad (who used to drink coffee before she came along with her health-food ideas.) She was wearing some kind of shapeless overalls, decorated with army fatigue colors in a swirly design, over top of a bright yellow T-shirt. Sun, slanting in the east window, flared in her unruly hennaed curls, and glinted on the tiny chip of diamond in her pierced nose. I knew, without looking, that her feet were bare and she hadn't shaved her armpits forever. So what did my dad — so wholesome and contented looking in his oxford pants, his brown moccasin loafers, and his polo shirts — see in her? She had no class at all. She was from a different planet than my glamorous mother.

We were pretty quiet while we ate, but as soon as the last pancake was finished, Dad teased us. "I guess birthdays mean presents. Have you seen anything lying around, Pearl?"

Pearl rose and started clearing the table, sun shining on her glasses and her grandmotherly, blue-rinsed hair. "There might be one or two things in the front room," she said.

I started to shoot my chair back but then I remembered about being Seriously Mature and slowed down, stacking some plates and carrying them to the dishwasher before following everyone else into the front room. Noah was already cutting paper off something with his pocketknife. It turned out to be a snorkel and mask from Dad. Dad always gives presents that are practical and outdoor-oriented; it must be why Noah is turning into such a man-of-the-woods kind of guy. Usually, Dad buys Noah and me different things, but this year he'd bought me a snorkel and mask, too.

"Thought you could use yours at camp, Noah," he said. "And Stella, you can pack yours for England."

England! Every time I thought about the trip Dad was taking Skye and me on next week, a current of excitement zinged through me. "Bet you wish you were coming," I teased Noah, "instead of portaging thousand pound canoes and risking Death By Bugs. Just think, while you're washing stinky socks in cold water, I'll be exploring King Arthur's Castle."

"Just think," responded Noah, "while you're standing around in crumbling ruins in the rain, I'll be cooking fresh-caught trout over a roaring fire."

"That is so totally unromantic," I told him.

Why would anyone rather go to an Ontario wilderness camp than fly to England? Dad, who teaches geography at Trent University, had some research to complete in London. He and I planned to stay with friends of his in the city for the first ten days. Skye, however, would head down to Cornwall by train as soon as we arrived, as she'd enrolled in an art course. So I'd have Dad to myself for the first ten days (discounting the fact I'd have to share him with stacks of learned papers)! After this, he and I would travel southwest by train to where Cornwall — the place my great-grandmother was born — juts its rocky toe into the Atlantic. We'd meet up with Skye for three and a half weeks before coming home. Dad had promised me miles of golden beaches, and secret coves where smugglers used to bring ashore brandy and French perfume at the dark of the moon . . . maybe I'd be inspired with new ideas for the short stories I like to write. And everyone at school would envy me in the fall, when I'd said I'd been surfing in Cornwall.

"Here you are, Stella," said Pearl, handing me a present just as my daydream reached the moment when I caught the perfect wave. The present was wrapped prettily in rose paper and tied with pink ribbons. Pearl knows perfectly well I've hated pink since I turned ten, but she still treats me like a little kid — a little girl. "Boys will be boys" she always says to Dad whenever Noah gets caught out, but when I get caught out, Pearl clucks and fusses about my terrible wild behavior. So un-girlish.

Anyway, I forgave her the pink ribbons this time when I opened the parcel; she'd ordered me a dress to die for from *Victoria's Secret*. It had spaghetti straps, and a slit up the back seam. The midnight-blue material shimmered when I moved it over my hands. "Oh, Pearl!" I said in delight, while Dad and Noah watched me with identical indulgent and baffled gazes.

Pearl had bought Noah a video game. He barely stayed long enough to open his present from Skye (a book about sketching wildlife) before leaping off to the rec room to plug the game into his Sega.

My present from Skye was a calligraphy pen, which is the kind of thing I expected since she's an artist. "You might like to use it for your poems," she said, and I had to suppress a scowl and thank her. Dad must have told her I write poetry, but my work is private. Only Ashley gets to read my poems and song lyrics on lazy afternoons when we've been swimming at the beach and come home to eat watermelon. Still, it was a pretty nice pen, accompanied by two bottles of colored ink and seven different nibs in shiny silver.

Pearl started bustling around folding up discarded paper after that, because she can't stand anything being in a mess, and Skye headed to town to open up her gallery. Dad and I strolled to the end of our driveway to fetch the mail. Our cat, Snowball, stretched out lazily on the lawn and watched us. The sun, higher now, shone on the front of the house: its pink granite walls, its green shutters, its little white sun porch. On either side of the porch, the red begonias Pearl had planted were brilliant splotches of color in hanging baskets. On either side of the driveway, the silver leaves of the cottonwood trees riffled in the breeze.

"A perfect morning," Dad said with satisfaction. "I'm canoeing in Eels Creek this afternoon. Do you want to come along?"

"No, thanks. Ashley's coming over," I replied quickly. It wasn't that I minded canoeing, but I knew if I went I'd be the only kid amongst a bunch of adults, all faculty from the university where Dad teaches. They'd spend the afternoon cracking jokes I wouldn't get, from literature like Spenser's *The Faerie Queen,* or else discussing ancient artifacts and rock stratum and the historical significance of somebody's theories.

Our mailbox is green, supported on an old cedar post, with wild white morning glory flowers twined around it. While Dad opened the flap and peered in, I watched our neighbor, John, approaching from down the road on his tractor. Blue smoke chuffed from the exhaust pipe.

"Morning," John called over the engine's throaty reverberation. "Gonna be a hot one. You gonna pick corn this year for me, Stella?"

"I'm going to be away — in England!" I shouted back, my face doing this big grin thing that I couldn't seem to control.

"Ah, well. You did a good job with the berries anyway," John roared. "You can send me a postcard!"

He trundled off, turning the tractor into the fields he rents from Dad, who obviously doesn't farm them himself. On weekends in June I supervise the stall at John's U-Pick strawberry patch, handing out baskets and taking money. Later in the summer, I usually pick corn to sell at the stall. My earnings buy things I want, like haircuts or a halter for Malibu, and usually I enjoy the work: the sweet smell of berries, the rustle of corn leaves. But now — England! I wouldn't have stayed to pick corn for triple pay. I hugged myself in anticipation. For five weeks, I was escaping from the quiet fields where nothing changed much season after season; from the boys I knew so well I could guess what they'd say before they opened their mouths; maybe even from myself, the confusing different people I held struggling within me.

"Look at this," said Dad, turning from the mailbox and passing me an envelope. The address was handwritten in blue ink, the letters shaky as though formed by someone with weak fingers. L. Trebilcock, Sunny Cottage, Looe, Cornwall, England, I read in the top left corner.

"Open it!" I said.

"Sure," Dad agreed. "It's probably from someone I contacted when I was searching for your mother's side of the family over there."

He pulled out a single sheet of thin, airmail paper covered in the same spidery writing and two photographs, which he passed to me. One showed an elderly lady by a cottage door; the second showed a group of three kids standing on a harbor wall with sailing boats in the background and a seagull flying overhead. Two of the kids were small, but the boy standing in the middle looked older than me.

"Who are they?" I asked.

Dad scanned the letter quickly. "It's from a distant cousin of your mother's," he said. "Lavinia Trebilcock. She's seventy-four and lives in north Cornwall."

I grimaced. She didn't sound too interesting. I imagined a boring visit in a small room with lace curtains and tea in china cups, while Lavinia went on about long-dead relatives and a clock ticked loudly on the mantel.

"How can she be so much older than Mom if they're cousins?" I asked.

"They're distant cousins," Dad repeated. "They're different generations. You know how it is with extended families: the oldest children in one branch can be much older than the youngest children in another branch.

"Lavinia's lost touch with any other family members," continued Dad. "Oh, wait, no, she still keeps in sporadic touch with another cousin called Janet. Janet and her husband are separated and Janet doesn't live in Cornwall anymore. But her son, Nicholas, still visits there occasionally in the summer. He's the boy in the middle of the picture, standing beside some neighbors of Lavinia's. He's fifteen . . . hmm . . . he'll be in Cornwall this summer staying with his father near Falmouth. She's given a phone number where we can reach them . . . says to visit her in Looe . . ."

I examined the photo with new interest. A black leather jacket was draped carelessly over one of Nicholas' thin shoulders, its collar pressed against his dark, untidy hair. His eyes, dark blue in a tanned face, seemed to stare straight at me and his expression was aloof, as though he was totally bored with little kids and Cornish harbors.

Maybe he surfs, I thought. Maybe he and I could surf . . . and afterward we'd stroll along the beach eating ice cream and then later we'd have a fire on the beach — no, a beach party and he'd introduce me to his friends — and then another day maybe we'd all play volleyball on the sand . . .

The airmail paper rustled crisply as Dad stuffed the letter back into the envelope. "Mind if I take a look?" he asked, and I reluctantly handed over the pictures.

"Well, this might be a bit of luck," Dad said. "Skye's art course is in Falmouth so we'll be in the area; maybe you can give this distant cousin a call. He'll be company for you since Noah is staying in Canada."

"Yes," I agreed, keeping my voice carefully neutral, but as I wandered back up the drive I kicked a white pebble ahead of me. My legs felt jittery with excitement. Wait until I told Ashley about my tall, dark Cornish cousin!

CHAPTER TWO

"Who's going to cook supper?" Ashley asked.

"Pearl," I replied, and we both glanced toward the verandah, where Pearl was reading the paper in a wicker chair. The verandah runs along the single-story addition at the back of our house. Dad had it built for Pearl to live in so she could have "some privacy and peace and quiet." I guess it can't be easy suddenly moving in with a family when you're used to living alone, and then having two energetic kids underfoot all the time. Pearl seemed to manage it pretty well, learning right away how to cook macaroni and cheese just the way that Noah and I, at age six, loved it.

"Is she making her Black Forest cake?" Ashley asked hopefully, swinging her heels against the cedar fence rail.

"I don't know," I said. "Just be so-o-o grateful that Pearl is cooking and not Skye. She'd make Thai something or other with weird spices. Why can't she cook normal stuff, like Pearl does: chicken pies, pizzas, spaghetti and meatballs?" I complained. "Everything Skye cooks has some exotic name: tahini, tabouli, jambalaya, bulgar . . . none of it even sounds edible. Just because she's traveled all over the world doesn't mean she can't cook normally, does it?"

I wiggled around on the top fence rail where we were both perching like swallows. Malibu's teeth made a peaceful sound in the pasture as they ripped up grass. Pearl's hollyhocks were in bloom along the fence line, and we had to be careful of them as we swung our feet.

"What does Noah think about Skye's cooking?" Ashley asked, and I gave her my best steely eyed *Tomb Raider* look. I was starting to think she might have ulterior motives in regards to Noah these days; she was always asking things about him.

"Noah's cool with it," I said. "All Skye's stories about shopping in the markets of Istanbul and Singapore just wash over him. Personally, I think they're totally boring. And Pearl's no help," I said moodily.

"What do you mean?"

"She just told me to eat with a grateful heart; said she herself was 'more than happy to have someone else show a little interest in the menu around here,'" I mimicked. Ashley giggled and I gave her another stern look. It didn't seem right for Pearl to side against me; I felt vaguely betrayed.

"Well, my mom has decided I should 'assist with domestic duties' — meaning I have to cook supper every third evening," said Ashley in disgust, rolling her eyes melodramatically. "It's totally dumb. I don't need to know about all that stuff yet! I'm still a kid!"

"At least you're a kid with a mom," I replied.

I hated it when Ashley criticized her mother, who was a really kind lady. How could Ashley grumble about a woman who'd stuck around long enough to teach her how to cook? How could she be so ungrateful? But then, I also hated it when Ashley went on about how great her mom was, or stuff they'd done together. I didn't want to be jealous of my best friend but sometimes I couldn't help the dark, twisting feeling in my chest that wrapped around my heart and squeezed it tightly. What was I supposed to tell Ashley in return when she shared her mother with me? What could possibly be of equal value?

Over the hill, somewhere in what Pearl calls "the back forty", a calf bawled for its mother. Malibu grazed up behind us and raised his muzzle, smearing grass foam on the sleeve of my black silk shirt.

"Come on," I said to Ashley. "Help me decide what to pack for England."

We slid down from the fence, hopped between the hollyhocks, and headed inside. "Dad says Cornwall has some of the best beaches in the world," I told Ashley over my shoulder as we clumped up the dim, cool stairs to my bedroom. "Teams from South Africa and Australia go there to compete in surfing contests . . . and Dad's promised to show me around London. We're going to ride a double-decker bus."

"Maybe you could catch a boyband concert," suggested Ashley.

"Yeah, that would rock!"

Ashley flopped onto my bed with friendly abandon and I threw open my closet doors. "Ta da!" I said dramatically, as though she hadn't already seen everything there was to see in there.

"I'm only taking my fave stuff," I told her. "Starting with my dress from Pearl, and that yellow bikini I bought last month. Oh, and my mom's flute so I can keep practicing."

"What kind of girls do you think Nicholas likes?" Ashley asked.

"Dunno," I muttered. "I could go for feminine — or tough." I slung a sundress over one shoulder and a pair of black jeans over the other.

"Let's see the picture again," Ashley said, and I slid it from the pocket of my silk shirt, where I'd put it earlier after borrowing it from Dad's desk. We bent over it, scrutinizing Nicholas closely.

"He's dreamy," Ashley said. "You have to write me every day and tell me what you're doing."

"The letters might get censored by British officials," I teased.

Ashley rolled her eyes. "Get on with your packing," she said.

I flapped a wrinkled sweatshirt at her, then dropped it onto my reject pile on the floor. Most of my other clothes were in the pile already: a sweater with fuzz balls on the sleeves, a dress too tight under the arms, a nerdy gray skirt with pleats, a pale blue shirt that I'd looked good in only when my hair was blonde last fall. I tossed the shirt to Ashley. "For you," I said. With her pale gold hair and her milky skin, she'd look just right in it. Half an hour later I was surrounded by rejects and threw myself on the bed by Ashley.

"Sometimes, being Seriously Mature is a lot of work," I complained.

"Umm," she said, staring out the window at Noah, who was bouncing a basketball around below his hoop. "I think I'll get a drink," she said, but she didn't fool me. She was going to accidentally engage Noah in conversation while looking for Pearl to ask her for some lemonade.

"Have a jolly time, old bean," I told her in my best British accent as she slipped out the door. What kind of an accent would Nicholas have?

I stared gloomily at the pile of rejected clothes, then pulled a photo album with worn covers from my bedside table and leafed through it slowly. The pictures were colored, so they seemed recent. There was our house in one of them, looking just like always: same pink granite and sun porch. If you didn't know better, you might think the photos were taken just last week. The trouble is, I do know better — these photos were taken in another lifetime. My mother's lifetime.

Lately, I've been getting this funny feeling that the people in my life are farther away than they used to be. Like we all used to be walking along some trail in the bush, jostling along it together, and now suddenly we're each on our own parallel trail. Dad's over there to one side of me, walking along thinking about Skye with that besotted smile he has when he looks at her. And Noah's off on the other side of me, on his own trail. He's thinking about beating the next level in a video game or making it onto the basketball team. I think he's walking in step with me, because we're twins, but every so often he goes behind a tree and I can't see where his feet are heading.

In science, my teacher said that everything in life is relative, and so I guess that's why it's easy to be aware of my mom these days. Now that everyone else seems farther away, it's not so hard to imagine her out there on a trail of her own, slipping through the trees to one side of me. She doesn't seem so far off even though she's been dead for eight years, since I was six. It was breast cancer; she was sick for almost two years. I sort of remember sitting on the end of her bed, but I can't remember her face. Only Pearl and my dad really remember her, the person she was. Pearl says she was beautiful and smart; Dad tells me she designed fashions for runway models.

The problem with Dad and Pearl as sources of information is that neither one is very talkative about my mother. Trying to get answers from them is like trying to catch wet frogs in long grass: at the last minute, they get away. Dad doesn't really talk about feelings; he doesn't remember the kinds of little things that are important. Well, he's a guy. So he focuses on practical, here-and-now stuff, like how to keep squirrels out of the bird feeder we built together in the fall or how to build a shoe rack into my closet. And if, when he's hammering away,

I say something casual like, "So what were my mother's favorite colors?" he'll grunt and shrug, mutter, "I can't remember," and say, "pass that screwdriver, will you please?" Once, when I pressed him for an answer, he sighed and told me there was nothing one could do about the past, one had to let it go and focus on what needed doing in the present. My dad, Mr. Handyman.

Pearl is sentimental. She likes happy endings in life. When she watches soap operas she turns a blind eye to all those evil characters scheming on stealing the heroine's man. Pearl's like a horse in blinkers: she ignores certain things as though this will make them go away, will wipe them off the planet. Then she can have the ending she wants.

Occasionally, Pearl reminds me that my name, Stella, means star and that it was chosen for me by my mother. Sometimes my mother said I was her star, sometimes she said I'd grow up to be a stunner, a star. She said I had star quality. This is what Pearl tells me when she's feeling especially grandmotherly and sentimental — as if she's handing me a happy ending.

The problem is, what did Mom think it took to be a star? Would she have approved of my modeling and singing lessons, the fact that I was learning to play her flute? What would she advise me to wear on a romantic holiday in the land of King Arthur? What would she herself have worn to meet a boy who was a stranger even though somewhere, way back, his blood was the same as hers?

I stared very hard at all the photos even though I knew their details by heart. I always think there are answers for me in that photo album, if only I could hear them. Here is my mother stepping out of a taxi: a long, elegant leg in suede pants, a hand with pink nail polish on the rim of the cab door. Here is my mother at the beach, her silk wrap blowing in the wind, her slender feet in white leather thongs. Here is my mother in an aqua suit with a short skirt and fitted jacket, talking to my father on the lawn of our house. Here is my mother looking perfect, glamorous, gorgeous. My laughing mother, the star in my sky, her smile reaching out to me across miles of elapsed time . . . her smile reaching me years after she has died. How can I ever live up to her expectations? Her memory?

I slid the album back onto the table by my bed and buried my face in my quilt. The late afternoon sun warmed my back and made me sleepy. Soon, Dad would be home for my birthday supper. Maybe I'd ask him to drive Ashley and me to town tomorrow, so we could go to the malls. Now I was fourteen, maybe he'd let me shop without Pearl. I'd buy sundresses, not the ruffled kind but the long, floating kind with slits in the side seams. New sandals. Baggy, Gap shorts for the beach. T-shirts striped in navy and white, like a French painter's smock. Which reminded me . . .

I felt under my bed for the most recent issue of *Vogue* and leafed through it. There was a whole article on French chic: haughty women with long braids sitting at café tables and lounging on the decks of sailing boats, their legs enveloped in swathes of tulle and gauze, or red leather, or silk. It was all so gorgeous and impractical. Had my mother designed clothes like these?

Distantly, downstairs, the telephone shrilled. I raised
my face from the magazine and listened. It kept ringing.
Pearl didn't seem to be answering it and Noah was outside. I could hear his basketball thumping on the gravel
by the pasture rail and Ashley's voice talking to him. The
answering machine will get it, I thought, but then I
decided it might be Dad calling about the birthday supper and I leaped down the stairs and grabbed the receiver
just before the machine cut in.

"Hello!" I gasped, fumbling the receiver to my ear.

"Stella?"

"Dad?"

His voice sounded funny: raspy, and as if he was far
away.

"Stella, I'm at the Civic hospital. I think I've broken
my leg so I might be here for a while. Canoeing accident.
Not sure about supper."

"Dad!" I gasped again. Something cold clutched
at my stomach. Words rolled around in my mouth, getting in each other's way, failing to come out. "Dad, are
you okay?" was all I could manage. (A majorly dumb
question.)

"The nurse wants me, have to go," Dad said. "Tell
Pearl, okay?"

"Yes. Dad —" but I didn't know what I wanted to say
and, anyway, he'd hung up.

"Noah!" I shouted, heading out the door in blind
instinct, heading for the other half of myself, those eyes
shaped like mine, those same freckles on the bridge of
the nose. "Noah! It's Dad — he's hurt!"

Abruptly, Noah caught the ball out of the air and

swung to face me, his runners grinding gravel. Noah is a practical person, not a dreamer like me. "What's happened? Where is he?" he asked. "Does Pearl know?"

It took us half an hour to reach town. Pearl drove with silent, single-minded concentration, her face as fierce as it can ever be. Behind us, the yard was silent but for a robin's song. The birthday meal was cooling on the stove; the cake sat in the fridge. Ashley had biked home after we'd all run outside, slamming shut doors that had been open all day.

As soon as Pearl parked the car in front of the hospital, Noah and I leaped from it and jogged up the steps to the helicopter pad. We crossed it at a run and dashed toward the automatic, sliding glass doors of the emergency department. They barely opened in time to admit us. The emergency was stuffy and crowded, full of anxious faces, softly crying children, wheelchairs in use or standing empty, waiting. We paused to let Pearl catch up to us and then we followed her to the reception desk. The nurse consulted a file, called back to another nurse, then told Pearl, "He's in the cast room. You'll have to wait here."

Noah and I slumped on the vinyl chairs and stared glumly at the floor. If Dad's leg is broken, I thought, will we have to cancel our trip to England? A wall of disappointment slammed into me — then I felt guilty. I was whole and well, and Dad was injured. What did a trip matter compared to Dad? *But I really want to go*, muttered a rebellious, obstinate voice deep inside me. I glanced sideways at Noah.

"Dad is more important," he said, reading my mind the way only he can do. I started reading his: maybe he wouldn't be able to go to camp now, if Dad couldn't drive him there the day after next. Which leg had Dad broken? How long would it take to heal? Would he walk with a crutch? What about his research?

"Maybe you can carpool to camp," I said softly to Noah. No such luck for me, no way to carpool across the ocean.

Beside me, Pearl rustled through the pages of *Chatelaine* in noisy anxiety. I tried to distract myself with the television perched on a table in the corner, but the show was some American thing about cops in a car chase. The commentator seemed to think he was at a sports game and keeping score in his fake, excited tone of voice. Dead boring.

We waited for what seemed about two days. My stomach kept growling and each time Noah's stomach growled in response. Pearl kept glancing fretfully at her watch and clicking her tongue. Every time anyone came down the hall, our three sets of eyes swiveled in that direction. Once, I got up and wandered around, staring at posters about medical care as if they were some kind of fascinating art on the wall. I could feel Pearl watching me over the top of her magazine.

"You look more like your mother every day," she commented as I sat down beside her again. "Same long legs, same hair."

Did this mean I was like her in other ways? I wondered. Did it mean I would have her shining successful glamour when I grew older? What did my father think when he looked at me — did he see her, like a ghostly image, in my face? Did he like being reminded, or did it mean only sadness for him?

Time dragged by as I pondered these questions, staring down at my toes, my nails slick with fluorescent polish.

At last, Dad was wheeled toward us by a black male nurse, his left leg was jutting awkwardly forward, huge in the plaster cast. His tanned face was pale and sweat beaded his forehead. With a pang I noticed the gray in his hair; suddenly he looked old.

"I can manage now," Pearl was saying, taking the wheelchair handles possessively from the nurse, almost pushing him aside. Noah gripped Dad by one arm, and I bent and kissed his cheek, feeling his slight stubble.

"Oh, Dad," I said, blinking away tears. "What happened?"

"Not quite sure," Dad said as Pearl wheeled him to the door, then went to fetch the car. "It all happened so fast. The canoe capsized in shallow water, rapids. Hadn't canoed that stretch before. My leg got caught under a rock. I would've been okay but then Fleming's canoe got out of control and went side on into me, knocked me sideways, and my leg snapped."

I felt cold all over, holding Dad's arm. Right then, wild horses couldn't have dragged the word *England* out of me. "Do you have a quarter?" I asked Noah, and he rummaged through three pockets in his baggy pants. "It's listed under Orion Gallery," he said, handing me the money.

"I know," I called back, heading for where I'd seen the

pay phones. After I dialed, the telephone rang and rang. Maybe I was too late and she'd already left. Oh, why hadn't I done this sooner? It was such a small thing to do for my father. Finally, she answered.

"Skye," I said. "Can you meet us at the house? Dad needs you. He's broken a leg."

I caught up with everyone in the parking lot where it was taking ages to maneuver Dad into the front seat of the car, even with the help of the male nurse who'd followed us out. Noah and I exchanged glances over the huge cast; we could read each other's eyes. Things are not looking good, we told each other silently. Then Noah stashed Dad's crutches in the trunk, and we both climbed into the back seat and headed home to our birthday cake and whatever might happen afterward.

CHAPTER THREE

Rats, rats. How did I get myself into this situation? "Don't give Skye any hassle," were almost the last words Dad said before I left home, but here was Skye giving me hassle (just like I knew she would) before we cleared the airport security. We weren't even out of the country yet!

It started when she walked through that kind of metal detector arch that airports use. I'd walked through first without problems and was just picking my bag and flute case off the conveyor belt when Skye stepped through, and the detector's alarm began beeping wildly. Immediately, a uniformed guard stepped forward holding some gadget.

"Lift your arms," he instructed curtly and began waving the gadget around her body. Sheesh.

I stared away, as if I was waiting for someone else and not Skye.

"Any change in your pockets?" the man asked, and Skye shook her head. By now, two more guards flanked her, and a line of impatient travelers craned their necks to see what was causing the holdup.

I stared at my new bag, tracing my fingertips over the circular pattern woven in golden straw. It was just like the bag the heroine carried around Italy in my favorite summer movie, *Gateway to Heaven*. When I risked a glance in Skye's direction, she was taking off her loose jacket of purple and red patchwork squares and handing it to a guard. I composed my expression into one of boredom and was careful not to meet Skye's glance in case she said anything to me and people figured out we were together. Now the guard was running his gadget over Skye's jacket.

"It's the hole in the lining!" decided Skye suddenly with a laugh. Unbelievable. She should have been frozen to the spot with embarrassment but, no, she was making a joke out of it. If the guards huddled around had been sheepdogs, they would've been growling. Only a moron would try to make them laugh.

Now Skye was fumbling with the jacket, pulling one pocket inside out to reveal ragged lining; she stuck her hand through a hole and withdrew several coins, wads of fluff, and a shriveled mixture of vegetable matter. "Here's the problem," she said. "Just a few nickels."

The guards bent over her hand.

"What's all this?" one asked suspiciously, waving a finger at the plant gunk.

"Bits of dried lavender," Skye said happily, holding it under her nose and inhaling. "Smell it. Lovely!"

The guards wrinkled their noses — who could blame them? — and tried to look as if they could tell the difference between pocket-lining mushed-up lavender flowers and weird psychotic herbs from the Amazon jungle. They must have decided not to display their ignorance because they handed Skye's jacket back to her and waved her brusquely toward her flight bag waiting on the conveyor belt. I swung my legs quickly away down the concourse leading to the gates. Let Skye catch up to me. I could feel all the other passengers' eyes burning holes in my back as it was. I didn't need Skye hurrying along beside me in her battered sandals and the shapeless purple dress that matched her old jacket, inhaling dried-whatever from one hand.

We had forty minutes to wait at our departure gate, so I opened a magazine and wondered if I'd made the right choice the day after Dad broke his leg.

Pearl had settled Dad in a chair in the front yard, in the shade of the cottonwood trees. "Stella," she had hollered toward where I was mooching around outside the barn, chewing grass and wondering if I dare ask anyone what was happening about our trip to England. "Stella, your father wants to talk to you."

I dropped the piece of grass and strolled around to the front, trying to look nonchalant, as if the thought of a trip to England was the very last thing in my mind. Dad grinned at me ruefully, his plaster leg stretched out to rest on a footstool and his crutches lying on the grass.

"It's going to take me awhile to get over this," he said, and I just nodded. "But that doesn't need to spoil your fun. The tickets are already fully paid for, so you can still go to England, although of course you won't see as much of London."

"I can't go alone," I said.

"Skye's offered to take you with her. She's still going to do the art course. You'll spend two days sight-seeing in London together and then take the train to Falmouth. You'll stay in the apartment I've rented there."

"I don't want to go with Skye!" I blurted out. "I want to go with you!"

"Well, that's not possible now," Dad said reasonably. "I'm sorry you won't see much of London, Stella, but I think you and Skye will enjoy Cornwall."

"I doubt it," I muttered, shredding the petals off a daisy.

"Pardon?"

"What am I supposed to do while Skye is painting?" I asked rebelliously.

"She's going to contact your mother's relations and see if you can spend time with them. She's also volunteered to check into singing lessons and modeling schools for you in Falmouth. Otherwise, I'm sure you'll find plenty to do, Stella. You're an independent young woman."

I knew, from his tone, that Dad's eyes were twinkling but I refused to look at him. I was super disappointed in him right then. How could he do this to me? I glared at my blurred fingers, twisting in the grass. If you cry I'll kill you, I told myself. Get a grip.

Dad sighed at my dismal response. "There's no reason you shouldn't still have a good trip," he said firmly.

"Except for Skye."

The words hung in the air outside my mouth, quivering in front of me, in front of Dad.

"You're being childish," he said sharply. "Skye is a warmhearted person — and patient with you, which is more than you deserve. If you can't manage to be mature about this change of plans, Stella, you can stay home and help Pearl out around here. I'm sure Skye would find the trip easier without you dragging your feet behind her."

The wind whispered through the cottonwood trees, and a dying begonia blossom fell from the hanging basket on the sun porch to land with the lightest of plops at my side. I stared at it, totally miserable. A little part of me knew that I was behaving badly and that Dad was right about Skye; another part of me felt plain mad about her existing in my corner of the universe. She irritates me, I thought stubbornly. Maybe I'd just stay home and pick corn and earn money, bike to the river with Ashley, lie on the beach while the boys we knew from school played volleyball. I'd show Dad I couldn't care less about going away.

I glanced at Dad. His face had a kind of gray look, and sweat was beading on his forehead the way it had the previous evening when Pearl wheeled him from the hospital. Remorse pricked me. He had enough problems without me being so whiny. What about his trip, his research? When he bent to reach for his crutches, I scrambled to help him.

"Time for some painkillers," he muttered, and I nodded miserably.

"Sit still, I'll fetch them with a glass of water," I said.

In the kitchen, letting the water run, I knew I really had no choice. I'd have to make the best of the altered plans and hope I could keep Skye and my Cornish cousins in separate boxes.

The week that followed passed quickly. Ashley and I shopped and packed and pored over Nicholas' photo. We decided he was brainy and artistic, played steel guitar, spoke French fluently, and would fall madly for me. I took Malibu for a last ride, and promised Dad that I'd behave, and waved Noah goodbye as he carpooled off to camp.

"This is a preliminary boarding call for those passengers needing assistance or with young children," crackled the PA system, and my head snapped out of my magazine. Soon it was time to thump down the echoing corridor to where the flight attendants waited just inside the plane doors with their smiles pinned in place.

I hoped that maybe there would be some problem with the seat allocations. "We're so sorry," one of the attendants would say to me. "We seem to have a seating problem. Would you mind moving?" And I'd end up half a plane length from Skye; so far away that I wouldn't be able to see even the top of her head. No one would know we were being forced to endure each other by a cruel twist of fate.

But no such luck. I slid into the window seat and Skye squeezed in beside me, while a stranger with a briefcase took the aisle seat in our row. We were as comfortable as sardines in the economy space that airplane designers think is suitable. Skye's knee was leaning against mine, so I shifted my position and stared out the little window at the runway.

A momentary pang shot through me as I thought of Dad sitting at home with his cast. Then sudden excitement gripped me as we taxied out, as the engines roared into full power, pushing my spine against the seat. The runway dropped beneath us, and I thought: This is it! I am really going to England! Dad had given me spending money so that I could visit some castles and beaches, and, somewhere in my future, Nicholas was waiting.

The plane tilted upward, Toronto dwindling below until it resembled a miniature world. Scarves of cloud wafted past the plane wings. I wiggled my toes happily in my new black leather thongs with three-inch platform soles of braided straw. My magazine lay unopened on my lap. Right now, I wanted to savor the experience of being lifted higher and higher. I stared out at lakes dwindling into puddles and clouds crinkled as cauliflower, while the flight attendants bustled around with the preoccupied politeness of waitresses at ground level.

About the time the plane leveled off at its cruising altitude of 34,000 feet, here's what I started thinking. Traveling is like leaving yourself behind and turning into a stranger, a person you're inventing as you go along. In that way, it's a lot like being a teenager. This can be kind of scary, like you've lost track of something way more important to your sanity than your locker key. But in another way, there's a feeling of freedom; you can choose any persona for yourself that you'd like. No one is going to tell you to be anything different, because no one around knows who you used to be. Think of the possibilities!

"Headphones?" asked the flight attendant.

"Yes, please," I said, and Skye rummaged through her shoulder bag (patches of velvet and corduroy sewn together) for some change. I plugged the headphone wires into the jack in the armrest, snugged the pads against my ears, and disappeared behind a music channel. Skye should get the message. If she hoped we were going to turn into buddies because we happened to be going to the same place on the same plane, she was doomed for disappointment.

I closed my eyes (blocking out that irritating edge of color from Skye's uncool dress) and went back to thinking about the possibilities of travel. Who might I be, at this moment? I pictured myself like someone in a movie: a girl at 34,000 feet, heading across the Atlantic ocean into tomorrow. Her straight hair is dark auburn, recently dyed and cut in a slightly diagonal line across her forehead and another diagonal line from front to back across her shoulders, making her look like that girl in the TV commercials for Femme Fatale shampoo. Her legs are tanned and smoothly shaved; a silver thumb ring shines on her right hand, and a silver bracelet, strung with amber beads, circles her left wrist. A T-shirt dress (goldenrod colored) drapes from her slim shoulders . . . she has traveled often, nothing amazes her, she handles life with aplomb. Her mother is a designer, they are on their way to Paris together for a summer show, her mother relies on the girl's opinions on new designs . . .

Suddenly, the bizarrely dressed woman on the girl's left intrudes with a comment.

"What?" I asked without opening my eyes.

"Supper," repeated Skye, and I jerked upright just in time to bump the edge of the tray that the stewardess was handing out. Skye managed to rip open her plastic packet containing a serviette before I did and mopped up the spilled water.

"Thanks," I muttered ungraciously. Pretty dorky, I told myself. Forget Paris and delicate operations like coaxing snails from their shells. I couldn't even manage an airline tray.

"What have we here?" asked Skye, peeling covers off her food. She sniffed appreciatively and tucked into the mixture of rice with peppers and some kind of beef strips in gravy. One thing I have to admit: she rarely complains about anything.

When we'd both finished the dessert of lemon sponge cake, I pulled a *Vogue* from my flight bag and started scanning the glossy pictures. Ads informed me that shoes with platforms were back in style, as I already knew. I wiggled my toes happily again in my own pair, beneath the instruction booklet on how to escape from a doomed plane. On the next page of *Vogue*, crop tops in sequins and ostrich feathers were being modeled by women with stomachs as flat as pool tables.

"What do you think about the fashion industry?" Skye asked.

I shrugged. Was she trying to start a conversation? She was supposed to be minding her own business, reading a paperback titled *The Zen of Creativity*, not peeking sideways into my magazine.

"Do you think magazines put pressure on women to look certain ways?" she persisted.

"Everyone wants to look their best, that's normal," I snapped.

"But who decides what's best?" she asked.

"People decide for themselves. It's a free country."

Skye pointed at the crop-top models. "How many young girls suffer from anorexia because they've grown up thinking they should look like this?" she asked. "Only one woman in hundreds of thousands has this body shape, Stella. Yet magazines tell us we should all look like this."

"So?" I said rudely.

"So magazines are fairytales for adults, Stella. These women don't exist. The photos are airbrushed. There's no lipstick in existence that doesn't smear, no skin cream that will banish wrinkles. The women in these photos only look glamorous for one instant in time, the moment it takes for the camera lens to open and close. The rest of the time they're just human like the rest of us — they get cavities in their teeth, they're cranky when they're tired."

You're just jealous because you're short and plain, I thought. "My mother looked like this," I said. "She looked wonderful all the time."

Skye stared at me for a long moment; her eyes seemed to be making some decision about me, but there was kindness in them. "I'm sure your mother's great personality was the most important thing about her," she said finally. "But that doesn't really show up in pictures, does it?"

Then she bent over her Zen book and began reading again. Had Dad shown her the albums, *my* albums of my

mother? How dare he? My mother's beauty and personality were none of Skye's business . . . although it was
true, what she'd said about things not showing up in pictures. Perhaps this was the answer I always looked for in
my mother's pictures — not how she achieved her
beauty, but who she really was. What lay beneath the
photos' glossy surfaces, the color of my mother's eyes,
the brightness of her smile? If she had lived, would I
have understood better — not only her — but myself,
and who I was and could be?

I sighed fretfully; thanks to Skye I wasn't in the mood
for *Vogue* anymore. I kept leafing through it anyway,
just to show her that she couldn't derail me whenever
she felt like it. But when the feature movie started rolling
credits, I slipped the magazine back into my bag. Skye
was already asleep, her Zen book wedged between us.
Night had claimed the world outside the plane, and I
glanced down through the clouds at the last sprinkling of
lights in Canada. Then I felt around in my flight bag for
a special shape: hard, slim, worn at the edges. The first
book I pulled out was the one I write my poems in, but
that wasn't what I wanted. I reached deeper and, from
between the folds of a sweater, I pulled it out: a dark
green book, its thick pages faded to ivory by time.

"I found this in your mother's stuff," my dad had
said, handing me the book after I dropped my suitcase at
the door. "It was a journal of your great-grandmother's,
Maggie Curnow McCormick. You might want to read it
now that you're going to Cornwall."

I vaguely remembered my great-grandmother: a thin,
tough woman who'd given me a bag of seashells when I

turned five. Ashley and I had used the shells as plates for teddy bear tea parties in the barn. Maggie died a few months later at the age of ninety-four. Her beloved husband, Harold, had already died peacefully in his sleep.

I'd always felt a bond with Maggie because she was red-haired, and a twin, and because she was an orphan. Not that I'm an orphan exactly, but losing my mother must count for something on the orphan scale. When my great-grandmother's twin, Thomasina, died on their ninety-fourth birthday, everyone said that Maggie gave up her own will to live. "She decided it was time to go," they said, when she died four days after her twin. Sometimes I wonder if this will happen to me and Noah.

Our Trip to Cornwall, June 1962 the first page of the journal was titled, in my great-grandmother's strong-looking writing. Underneath this was pasted a photo with the caption *St. Ives.* In the picture, Maggie and Harold were standing on a beach. Behind them, a harbor wall was a solid stone finger supporting a white light-house. Bright boats tipped drunkenly on rippled sand. Harold, my great-grandfather, was smiling behind his moustache but my great-grandmother's expression was not clear: was she laughing or crying?

The past is another country, one I never expected to return to, I began to read on page two of the journal. *Cornwall is my past, a vague memory of white sand and thrashing sea, the place where my childhood security was shattered by the death of my parents, the place from which I had to go forth and shape a new life, learning to let things go before I could claim my future.*

As the Boeing droned toward a pink dawn over the

Irish Sea, I raced through Maggie's journal, ignoring the movie's flickering light and the tired itch behind my eyelids. I was sure there were answers for me in this journal. Perhaps I would not understand them until I reached Cornwall, with its cold green waves and Iron Age forts, its dark, romantic history.

CHAPTER FOUR

"What do you think?" Skye asked.

I glanced at the brilliantly dyed, sarong-style skirt she was holding by the hanger and draping against herself, and shrugged. "Looks like your style," I replied, which was not necessarily a compliment. I can be diplomatic.

"I could use my 'mad money,'" she said. Before I rolled my eyes, I turned away so she wouldn't notice. Then, before I had time to gloat over my mature ability to show consideration, I had to leap backward.

"Whoa!" said Skye, grabbing my arm. I pulled away from her strong grip and we both stared after the car as it continued down the narrow, cobbled street. Ahead of the car, pedestrians jostled for safety on the ribbon of sidewalk; behind it they spilled into the street again. Falmouth had certainly been built for horses, or seamen on foot, not cars.

While Skye tried to decide whether the sarong was the one perfect thing to buy with her "mad money," I wandered on. It was only our second day in Falmouth and we had spent yesterday unpacking in the apartment Dad had rented over the Internet and buying food. Today, Skye had said we needed to "get out and find our bearings," and we were starting with the main street.

Dark alleyways funneled to the harbor, where fragments of sea glittered and red ferryboats bustled around. Outside a produce shop — a greengrocer's I had learned to call it — oranges and melons were piled in tempting pyramids. Even more tempting were the bakery shop windows with their trays of chocolate eclairs, jelly rolls, and cream puffs. How did English people stay slim? I would be a total pig if I lived here.

"Hungry?" asked Skye at my shoulder.

"Yes. I know it's only eleven-thirty, but I'm starving!"

"It's the sea air. Let's buy pasties."

"What?" I asked.

"Cornish national food," she replied. "The women used to bake them for their menfolk to eat down in the tin mines. They're delicious."

Coming from a woman who ate stuff with unpronounceable names, this was not reassuring. I cast a longing glance around for a hamburger-and-fries kind of place, but nothing was in sight. I followed Skye past The Grape Inn, its window boxes spilling over with geraniums and ivy, a waft of smoke and chatter spilling from its open door. At the end of the street, a stern looking church with a heavy gray tower blocked our view.

Although people around me were talking in English, I was constantly aware of being in a foreign country. Even the air seemed different: soft, and somehow filled with more smells than the air back home. Right then, I could smell cooking oil, and flowers, and the salty, weedy tang of the sea. Cobblestones were knobby under my feet. On either side of the treeless street, tall, old buildings stood joined together in rows.

"Here we are," said Skye, stopping in front of a store called The Oggy Oggy Pasty Shop. Pieces of golden pastry, folded over some kind of filling, lay on trays.

"What do they taste like?" I asked nervously.

"Like holidays and adventure and your own history," she said, pushing open the door. Weird. Was she going to talk like this inside the shop? I paused, uncertain whether I wanted to follow her in. "Come on!" she called, and my stomach rumbled, telling me to get a move on. The air drifting through the open door smelled savory.

It turned out that you can eat pasties while walking along, holding them by one end inside a paper bag. The pastry was flaky and light, the filling was meat and parsley, onion and potato. I gobbled mine greedily, and Skye just smiled at me and refrained from saying anything annoying, like "I told you so." Maybe we could make this trip work.

After we'd eaten, Skye brushed pastry crumbs from her "Women of the World Unite" T-shirt and disappeared into a gallery. I crossed the road and bought a special

postcard for Ashley. Actually it was more like six postcards all joined together in a strip that folded into a
concertina for mailing.

Later, after Skye had gone to her afternoon art class,
I lay on the little balcony outside our apartment and
wrote on the back of the cards with the pen Skye had
given me for my birthday.

*Dear Ashley, England is cool! Our flat (apartment
to you) has a view over the harbor to a lighthouse.
Skye and I have our own rooms — just as well since
she's using the front room for a studio and it's full of
paper & easel & paints. I've been very well behaved
and we haven't had any fights (yet). We spent two
days in London and rode on red buses and dragged
around art galleries for HOURS. I bought a pair of
earrings but Skye didn't buy anything. She has this
"mad money" that she's been saving for the trip. She
can't decide what to spend it on because she wants
to buy "one perfect thing." Must suck being poor.
I am taking singing lessons on Thursdays with a
woman whose studio used to be a sail-mending loft.
She has snow-white hair and makes me sing way
harder stuff than Mrs. Robertson at home. We're
doing opera songs. This afternoon I am going to
meet Nicholas!! His dad is driving into town to get
me. They live by the sea. I'm going to wear my
black T-shirt dress. You're right — it makes me
look older. Not sure you were right about curvaceous (I'm too skinny) but it does bring out my best
qualities. Wait for my Next Installment! Don't show*

*my letters to anyone else. Hope you're having a
jolly time (as the Brits say).*

Love Stella xxxxxxx

*P.S. Trains here have two kinds of coaches: First
Class (costs more) and Second Class. In London we
got into First Class with the rich people by mistake
and the ticket collector made us move into Second
with the plebs. We had to drag ALL our luggage
from the racks and move it too. I nearly DIED of
embarrassment!! Skye just laughed, even though it
was her fault we'd sat in the wrong place. Doesn't
anything get to her?*

Love S xxxxx

When I went out to wait for Nicholas' father, I slid the
postcard through the slot of a red letter box. Skye had
told me to wait outside for Richard so that he wouldn't
have the hassle of finding a parking space. I felt stupid,
like everyone would wonder who I was waiting for or
why I was standing there in one spot. I hoped Richard
wouldn't be late; on the phone he'd told Skye he would
collect me at two o'clock.

At least, while I waited, I could be glad I was looking
Seriously Mature. My hair was washed and it brushed
softly against my cheeks with each flurry of sea wind.
My black T-shirt dress, with bare back and crossover
straps, matched my black platform thongs. Around my
throat I'd fastened a choker of black beads shaped like
hearts, and my golden straw bag was slung over one
shoulder with my bikini, a towel, and sunscreen in it. I

figured I was somewhere between tough and feminine, and definitely rating high on the Cool Chic scale. And my black dress would match Nicholas' black leather jacket.

People kept jostling me on the narrow corner, and I had to keep stepping back into the doorway of a secondhand bookshop. Cars sometimes drove right onto the pavement as they edged past each other. When a car stopped in front of me, I was daydreaming about boats with romantic white sails. Somehow Nicholas and I might find ourselves together in one . . .

Barp!

A horn made me jump. I glanced at the low sports car, with its roof off and a male driver at the wheel, and then my gaze skittered away again. What would I wear in a boat? White espadrilles . . .

"Stella?"

I jumped again and glanced back at the car. "Stella?" the driver repeated. I stared at him uncertainly. This was Nicholas' father?

"Hope I'm not late! Nicholas is waiting at home," he said, leaning over to open the passenger door.

This was Nicholas' father! I leaped toward the car, bumping into a lady with shopping bags, blood rushing into my face. What a moron I was, dreaming on a street corner!

"Stella, a bright new star in the Cornish sky," Nicholas' father said warmly when I'd finished sinking into the cream leather seat. He grasped my right hand in his tanned one and a fresh wave of heat surged into my cheeks. I hid behind my hair, fumbling with my seat belt and blocking out his lean, tanned face and teasing blue eyes. His dark untidy hair — swept back, curly at the collar — looked like Nicholas' hair in the photo. He released the clutch, shifted into first, and the car prowled forward up the narrow street.

"Call me Richard and this is Blondie."

I let out a nervous exclamation as something cold and wet nudged my cheek. When I turned, the dog seemed to be laughing, her tongue flapping and her long coat rippling. "Oh, she's beautiful!" I said.

"Afghan hound, most elegant kind of dog alive," Richard said. "You like animals?"

"Yes, especially dogs and horses."

"You and Nicholas should go hacking," he said, shifting gears again as we shot through a tiny space between a delivery van and a parked car. Maybe he felt me flinch because he laughed and sped forward even faster. "This car has no fear!" he shouted over the wind and, when I looked back at Blondie in the tiny rear seat, her ears were streaming backwards and her almond eyes gleamed.

"What's 'hacking?'" I asked.

"Trail riding to you," said Richard. "You'm going to need an interpreter 'ere weth we, m'dear," he teased with a Cornish accent. His shirt, unbuttoned halfway down inside his black leather jacket, flapped in the wind. Sunlight glinted on his expensive gold watch and the gold rims of his shades.

"I'm pleased you've come," he said. "Nicholas is moping around on his own. He doesn't have any mates here since his mother took him to live upcountry. Wait until he sees what a bird I'm bringing him!"

I giggled (not Mature of me) and glanced at the landscape blurring past. We had climbed a long hill out of Falmouth and were heading southwest through rolling farmland. High stone hedges, starred with wild flowers, blocked our view but at intervals a gateway let me catch glimpses of blue sea on the left. Overhead, the crooked branches of ancient trees met to form a leafy roof so that the road seemed to twist through a green tunnel. Shadows and sun flew across us. Blondie poked her long, slim nose into my ear, and Richard glanced at me when I laughed.

"She's full of tricks, just like her namesake. You listen to Blondie in Canada?"

Before I could answer, he turned on the CD player and the rock group's driving beat filled the rushing air.

My face stretched into a grin; I wanted to holler and sing with excitement. This was living! I wished Ashley and the kids at school could see this scene, like a clip from a movie: me with a stylish haircut whipped by wind, riding in an expensive silver car with a golden dog and a man in black leather at the wheel. Can you dig it? my voice asked Ashley in an imaginary soundtrack. It was an image I loved — and this was only the beginning. Wait until I met Nicholas!

Richard slowed the car and swung through a narrow gap flanked with lichen-crusted granite posts. The lane was so narrow that grass on the hedges whispered against the car. "Keep your arms inside," Richard warned me.

Suddenly the hedges ended and we drove across rough, open ground. Glittering blue sea filled my eyes; sunlight fell hotly across my shoulders. On prickly bushes, golden flowers filled the air with a smell like coconut.

"Tez the furze, me 'andsome," Richard teased me again with a thick accent and gestured toward the bushes. "Gorse to the English, furze to the Cornish."

The car nosed downhill toward thick shrubbery; suddenly we were in a gravel turnaround beside the white stucco walls of a house.

"Welcome to Rose Mullion," Richard said as we climbed out of the car. "Nicholas should be around somewhere. I've got some calls to make; if you walk down through the garden, you'll find a path to the beach. Watch for the cliff edge; it's a long way to fall."

He disappeared through the back door and I followed Blondie around to the front of the house where large windows looked out to sea. The garden sloped downhill, with terraces of shaggy grass and low stone walls between masses of overgrown shrubs. A prickly plant looked like a desert aloe. Elegant pampas grass and small palm trees added an exotic touch. There was a private, secret feel to the garden despite the wind blowing in from the wide-open sea.

My heart beat in my throat. Talk about feeling alone. Where was Nicholas? Didn't he want to see me? Should I shout his name? "Good girl," I said to Blondie, running her silky coat between my fingers. She bounded ahead of me like a deer. When I followed, I found a steep, narrow path winding down the side of the cliff. I began to scramble down, slipping and sliding on my platforms. Finally I had to stop and take my shoes off, then pick my way gingerly with bare feet. The path ended in craggy rocks.

"Totally awesome," I whispered in delight, looking

down. Below the rocks, a cove shaped like a sickle moon filled the space between two rocky headlands. Between these arms, the cove was secret and warm. A slow swell of deep water sighed in to wash the white sand and gray pebbles. A sleek white sailing boat rode the green waves, dipping and swinging on her anchor. It looked like the perfect setting for a story; maybe I'd use it next time I wrote one.

I looked for a way down, then noticed a strange U-shape cut through the solid rock, as if someone had scooped it out with a huge knife. "Dynamite, more likely," I said aloud, and Blondie tilted her head at me. I climbed down through the cut, avoiding green weed, and jumped onto the beach. Ahead, Blondie ran to the water's edge and barked. I looked up in time to see a Windsurfer's yellow sail appear from behind one headland. A tall boy in a neon lime-green wet suit balanced below the sail.

"Nicholas!" I shouted and waved my straw bag in the air.

CHAPTER FIVE

The boy in the wet suit did not respond to my shout. Of course, I realized he couldn't let go of the sail boom without falling into the water. He could have shouted, though, or looked over at me. Maybe he hadn't heard me. Should I shout again? I gnawed my lip, then opened my mouth to call — but shut it again. Maybe this wasn't Nicholas? I felt dorky, standing staring at whoever-he-was as he skimmed across the mouth of the cove. At the far side, as he neared the rocks, he did some fast, complicated maneuver and the board and sail whipped around. He skimmed back across the cove, legs flexed and bare feet wet on the board. I risked giving another wave but couldn't tell if he was looking at me or not.

I pretended not to care. Nonchalantly I strolled down the beach, stopping to look at pebbles as smooth as candies and the red claw of a crab. When I reached the rocks on the far side of the cove, I discovered a boathouse built against the base of the cliff. I peered inside; folded sails were draped over rafters, and two small sailing boats lay on the shingle of gray and white stones. Below the boathouse, a zodiac, inflatable with an outboard engine, lay on a concrete slipway. I scrambled onto the rocks beside it and began to poke around in tide pools. They were filled with crystal-clear water and lined with pink weed-like coral, amongst which spiral shells nestled. Golden weed, like hair, drifted on the surface.

The sudden crunch of steps on the shingle alerted me. I straightened up, the ends of my hair dripping. The boy had beached the Windsurfer. I watched while he pulled it into the boathouse, then I jumped down onto the sand and strolled casually after him, holding myself tall and brushing my hair off my face with what I hoped was a careless, sophisticated gesture.

"Nicholas?" I asked the boy, when I reached him.

He squinted blue eyes against the light and glanced at me ever so briefly. There didn't seem to be any warmth in his eyes, none of the welcoming brightness I had anticipated. His look was aloof, the same as in the photo, but I was not a boring little kid. Why did he look at me like that?

"Yeah, I'm Nicholas," he said flatly.

"I'm Stella. I think we're sort of cousins, distant cousins."

Would we shake hands? I half-extended mine but he

was busy with the wet-suit zipper and my hand flapped around like a fish. I folded my arms over my chest. Nicholas began to peel the wet suit off; he was brown with thin, strongly muscled limbs. Moving into the boathouse, he hung the suit over a rafter, beside the sails. Outside again, he began to walk across the beach without glancing at me. I hurried to catch up.

"This place is awesome," I said. "Is it your dad's private cove?"

He nodded, his tousled hair falling over his eyes, but didn't say anything.

"What is this?" I asked as we scrambled up the passage cut through the rocks. "Did your dad make it?"

"It's old. Smugglers used it for transporting stuff up the cliff."

"Really?" A thrill tingled through me. I stopped to gaze down and imagine the cove in darkness: the slow dip of oars as the boat came in, the men wading into the surf to wrestle the barrels ashore, the donkeys waiting to carry them up the cliff while the customs men hunted through the heather with muskets . . .

A dislodged stone bounced past, and I realized that Nicholas had gone on without me and was already far above. Slipping and panting, I scrambled after him but didn't catch up until the top of the garden where he was having a drink from an outside tap. I slipped my feet back into my sandals.

I didn't know what to say. Something was wrong, or was I just imagining his unfriendliness? "It's hot, eh?" I asked, smiling. (Impressive conversation opener; really witty, Stella.)

Nicholas nodded without a smile and stared moodily down the garden. Silence stretched between us.

"What do you want to do?" he asked at last, and I shrugged nervously.

"May as well go in," he muttered, already turning away. I followed him to a side door. Inside, the house was filled with slanting sun. The slightly dusty furniture was all antique: chairs with curved legs and padded seats, a heavy sideboard, a huge mahogany table. Persian rugs glowed with brightly colored patterns of trees and birds. A stone fireplace stood cold and empty.

In the kitchen, Nicholas had the fridge door open and was scooping cake into his mouth. I sat down on a wooden chair and pretended not to notice that he hadn't offered me any. Finally, he did.

"Cake?"

"Yes, please," I said, much too eagerly and brightly. Oh, joy. I was like a little dog, waiting for crumbs of friendliness to fall, wagging my tail gratefully. My toes curled uncomfortably in my sandals. I smoothed my dress over my knees to calm myself and munched the cake that Nicholas passed me on a white plate.

Sudden movement by the door made me glance up; a woman was standing there, with a startled expression. Her flower print dress and fuzzy cardigan looked old-fashioned, and her hair was hidden under a dowdy scarf.

"Oh," she said, and her hand fluttered to her mouth. There was something funny about her accent; even the one word hadn't sounded English. Quickly she disappeared back down the hall.

"Who's she?" I asked curiously.

Nicholas stared at his plate. "Some creepy friend of my dad's," he replied grudgingly. Sheesh, I thought. Trade secrets. What was the matter with this guy?

"Is she visiting?" I asked, but before Nicholas could answer, Richard strode in.

"Oh, here you are," he said. He swiped a piece of cake from Nicholas' plate. "No more complaints of boredom from you," he said to Nicholas. "What do you think of your cousin? Should keep you occupied for the summer, you lucky bloke."

He swiped more cake, ignored Nicholas' dark scowl, and sent me a wink.

"Peter will drive you back at five, Stella," he said. "I've got to go out for a while. Make sure you come again soon. I'll have to take you both out sailing."

"Who's Peter?" I asked Nicholas after his father left.

"Dad's lorry driver," he replied, which was as clear as mud to me. I was too proud to ask for a further explanation. With a sinking heart, I heard Richard's silver car purr into life and then the sound fade away.

Nicholas slid his plate into the sink. "Come on," he said, and I followed him into the front room where he slouched in a chintz sofa and began to play a video game.

I watched the gun swiveling at the bottom of the screen, nosing its way toward danger and bloodshed. "Perfect Dark," I said, hoping he'd be impressed that I knew. But his eyes never flickered from the screen. I walked to the window and stared out at the sea beyond the sloping garden. A fishing trawler was churning westward, trailing a white V of waves. Sadly I thought of the

secret cove below the garden and wished that I was
down there with someone fun, that we were laughing
and chasing each other over the rocks and finding shells
in pools, and that I could learn to windsurf.

I sneaked a glance at Nicholas; out of the sun, his eyes
looked dark and sad — or was it angry? A lock of hair
fell forward along the straight line of his jaw. He was
dreamy, just like Ashley had said, but it didn't matter
because he didn't like me. What had I done wrong?

What stupid, mindless violence, I thought sourly,
watching Nicholas' assassins leaping around on the television screen. Nicholas didn't seem half as mature as
I'd imagined he'd be from his photo. But being sarcastic
didn't make me feel any better.

Wordlessly, I let myself outside and spread my towel
on the grass beneath a palm tree. Far below, waves
sighed soothingly on the rocks. I pressed my face against
my arm and waited for five o'clock, wishing I had a
book to read. At five to five, I strolled around the house
to the gravel parking space and met Peter.

He was a heavyset man with an earring, a tattoo of a
curvaceous mermaid on his biceps, and a flashing smile
in a black beard. He looked like a pirate (or a smuggler).
The "lorry" he drove me home in was a miniature transport truck. The cab had a bench seat, and behind the cab
was a big rectangular box without windows, for transporting stuff. "Richard Trenoweth, Fine Antiques" was
painted on the white sides.

"Does Richard have a store?" I asked Peter as we
rumbled out the lane.

"Es, up to Truro," Peter agreed.

I didn't think his Cornish accent was put on to tease me. "Are you going to the store now?" I asked.

"The shop? No, 'eading for Plymouth, m'dear. Go all over we do, buying and selling. Go upcountry all the time."

"Upcountry?"

"Over the Tamar River, into England."

"Isn't Cornwall part of England?" I asked.

Peter gave a barking sound, like a laugh that might bite. "Cornwall tezn't England, tez a separate place," he corrected me. "And too full of bleddy foreigners all buying 'oliday cottages. If we 'ad our own government 'ere, like we ought to, t'would be different. They foreign chaps up in London don't give a tinker's damn about we down 'ere."

The mermaid on Peter's biceps gave a muscled writhe of her tail. Not a combination to meet in a dark alley, warned the goose bumps on my neck. Was I in the category of "foreigner"? Peter, I suspected, was what my history teacher would call a nationalist.

"Where do the foreigners come from?" I asked.

"London, Manchester, Leeds, Liverpool . . . all over. Emmetts," he spat.

"Pardon? Emmetts?"

"Ants, tourists. Cornwall should be for the Cornish, same as tez always been. We make our own rules down 'ere. Stuff the English."

I tried to look inconspicuous, not even flickering my eyelashes or moving a single toe as I stared at the hedges flying past. If I breathed quietly, maybe Peter wouldn't notice that a real, live emmett was sitting in his truck.

Time for a change of topic, I thought anxiously. But what topic? My brain seemed to be taking its cues from my eyelashes; not a single helpful thought twitched in it. Then Peter spoke again.

"Know all they places upcountry I do, drive the van all over."

"Does Richard go too?"

"Depends. If there's sailing on, 'e do stay 'ome and sail. If tez no sailing to be 'ad, 'e do tour all the auctions and estate sales. Sells stuff in London, see?"

"Where does he sail?"

Peter shot me a sudden keen look that seemed to search me to the bone. He wasn't grinning. His beard bristled at me, like the back of a dog that senses trouble. "What do ee know about the sea?" he asked belligerently. "Tez a cruel master. There are more shipwrecks round Cornwall than ee can imagine — big boats and small, all gone to the bottom for the fish to live in."

I shivered. The wind, coming through the open windows, ran over me with an edge like a razor blade, like a deep current from the bottom of an ocean littered with skulls. I rolled up my window as Peter eased the van down into Falmouth's narrow streets. He stopped near the water's edge, outside the old warehouse converted to apartments that Skye and I were staying in. Converted for the emmetts, I thought uneasily.

"Thanks for the ride," I said in my politest voice, the one I save for teachers when they're deciding whether to give me a detention or a simple warning. I suspected that, in Peter's scheme of the world, I was even worse than an English foreigner. But when I'd climbed from the truck's high step onto a sidewalk spattered with seagull lime, his grin flashed at me like a lighthouse beacon.

"Cheers then, love!" he called, shifting the gears into first.

Antiques, I thought as I climbed the stairs to the third floor. That was where the money came from for the silver car and the white sailing boat and the house on the cliffs.

Maybe Nicholas was just a spoiled rotten rich brat.

I pushed open our apartment door and stepped inside. Late sunlight poured through skylights in the steeply pitched roof. On the front room wall, someone had indulged their decorating flare by draping a fishing net and some plastic crabs in a graceful swag. For the dumb emmetts, I thought.

"Hi! How was your afternoon? What are your cousins like?" Skye asked, padding around barefoot in front of her easel and looking at her painting from different angles. I didn't know why she bothered; from any angle it was a wild swirl of colors, a picture of nothing recognizable. She said it was a landscape.

I had my story ready — it was not untrue, but it wasn't the truth either. No way was I admitting to Skye that my tall dark cousin had ignored me all afternoon. "They have a sports car!" I told her brightly. "And a gorgeous house on the cliffs with a path to a secret cove. Richard sells antiques. He's rich. They have a big sailing boat and two small ones and a Windsurfer. Nicholas uses it. And they have a beautiful Afghan hound called Blondie, like the rock star."

"Umm."

Was Skye even listening? She was staring at her painting, and then darting in and adding flourishes and blobs of color. It was all executed at random as far as I could tell. But she had been listening. "Sounds like a nice lifestyle," she said. "But what about your cousins? When you meet someone, Stella, you have to look further below the surface than their lifestyle. What kind of people are they?"

My cheeks flamed, partly with embarrassment (because I couldn't tell her what kind of person Nicholas was) and partly because I was irritated by her. She didn't have to lecture me — I wasn't some dumb little kid! Don't give Skye any hassle, warned Dad's voice in my head, so I bit my lip and peeled an orange while counting to ten. Then I said, "Richard is really fun, he teases me. He puts on this Cornish accent. And Nicholas is . . . athletic."

And he's a stuck-up jerk, I added inside my head. I was so disappointed. What was I going to do for four and a half weeks, besides singing lessons on Thursdays? I'd just have to mope around on my own, reading magazines on the balcony and practicing my flute while Skye went off to her painting workshops with some world-famous artist. I would be bored and lonely and time would drag past. I wish I hadn't come, I thought. What a waste of summer. It's not fair!

Skye glanced at me and I quickly stuck an orange segment into my mouth and made a disgusting, stretched-out-of-shape face to cover my gloomy look. Maybe she caught the tail end of it anyway, because she set her palette down on the couch (which was draped artistically in an old sheet to protect it from flying paint), and said, "Come on. Let's go and buy fish and chips for supper."

We walked to the nearest chip shop. While we waited in line, Skye said, "I called your mother's cousin, Lavinia, today."

Oh, joy, more charming relatives. "And?" I asked.

"She'd love to see you but she's just recovering from pleurisy, and next week she has guests visiting. It seems she has no car so it's difficult for her to come to Falmouth. I promised we'd take the bus up to Looe to visit her sometime before we leave Cornwall. In a few weeks' time."

"Whatever," I agreed morosely, shuffling a step forward and staring at the dull brown jacket of the woman ahead of me in the line. The thought of a visit to Lavinia did not interest me now any more than it had when Dad first mentioned her — it certainly didn't catapult me out of my self-pity. Unless, I thought as I shuffled forward another step, Lavinia had known my mother well. Were there things about my mother that Lavinia could tell me?

Chapter Six

I felt sorry for myself for the next four days, busing alone across town and lying on the beach at Gyllyngvase. All around me little kids played naked, with sand sparkling on their chubby white bums. Groups of teens loitered outside the beach café, eating soft ice creams called Whippies and drinking pop from cans. I gazed across at them longingly. Did they think I looked interesting and mysterious, all alone with my headphones on and my back getting browner between the yellow top and bottom of my bikini? If I was in a movie, the camera would zoom in on me slowly as they started watching me. But this wasn't a movie; all they did

was walk past, too deep in conversation to send me even
a glance. Their feet kicked up a fine spray of sand that
itched on my bare back. Talk about being left in the dust.
I buried my nose in my poetry journal and composed
lines swollen with tragic feelings.

Then on the fourth evening, the phone rang in the
apartment while Skye was dabbing away at another
nothing-less canvas.

"Can you get that, Stella?"

Like it would be for me; the phone here was never for
me. Only Skye's artsy friends called, to discuss gouache
and egg tempera and the quality of Cornish light and
exhibitions with weird names like *The Tao of Flotsam*.

"Hello?" I said.

"Hello, this must be Stella. When are you coming out
to see us again?" asked Richard. "Are you finding things
to do in town?"

"I'm just hanging out," I said smoothly, like the apartment was full of my friends with their fave CDs and lots
of junk food to munch on. I wished.

"Catch the Maen Porth bus from outside Falmouth
Post Office and ask the driver to let you off near the
Rose Mullion lane," Richard suggested. "How about
tomorrow? Come for lunch."

"Umm, well . . . okay I guess," I said. "See you."

I strolled onto the balcony so I wouldn't have to
answer Skye's questions. I had to think. Was this lunch
thing Richard's idea or Nicholas'? Why hadn't Nicholas
called me himself? Was he shy?

I stared moodily across the harbor, watching a huge
black-and-yellow tug sweep upstream into the mouth of

the Penryn River. Small sailing boats dashed around like butterflies, and a Navy frigate poked its sharp, threatening bow out from the dockyards.

If I didn't go to lunch, what were my options for tomorrow? Watch boats. Wander around downtown. Watch music videos. Be bored. Go and wander around Henry VIII's castle on the headland by myself. Check out the Leisure Pool.

But if I went? An image of myself in the silver car flashed through my head. Me lying under a palm tree in the secret garden. Me windsurfing in the cove. Richard teasing me. Maybe he'd take us sailing. I imagined myself lolling in the cockpit, like one of the French models in last month's *Vogue*. Cool stuff.

Okay, so maybe Nicholas was having a bad day when I arrived. That happens to everyone. Maybe he deserved another chance. This time, I'd wear something different. Perhaps the black look had been uncool. How did I know what Brit boys liked?

Pigeons wheeled overhead as I crossed the square the next morning, heading for the bus. More pigeons fluttered on the pavement at my feet, and a seagull with a sardonic expression watched me from the top of a garbage can.

"Put the wrapper in the rubbish bin," said a voice behind me, and I turned in time to see a child run over and drop some paper into the garbage. Rubbish bin, I thought with a smile. Richard was right about my needing a translator.

I climbed the narrow spiral of steps to the top deck of

the bus and sat near the front. From this height, I could see right over the hedges as we lurched along country roads. Clumps of white flowers, like Queen Anne's Lace, and starry pink flowers waved in the hedges. Cows grazed methodically in the sunshine.

The bus driver let me off at the lane to Rose Mullion and I started walking. I noticed how secret the house was; even from the lane I couldn't see it. Its roof and walls were hidden by a swell of land and the thick shrubbery that grew around it. As I walked, a skylark trilled sweetly overhead, and the coconut smell of furze wafted around. I began to feel more optimistic.

It was such a beautiful morning; surely Nicholas would be in a better mood? And I was wearing white Bermuda pants with a lime-green T-shirt, and a matching necklace and bracelet set of enameled daisies, and white sandals with ankle laces. If I'd been in a photo shoot for a magazine, I'd have been looking just right. If my mom had been around, her face would've lit up when she saw me. She'd have said, "Girl, you're looking like a star."

I imagined myself posed nonchalantly in a gateway, while a horse hung its head over my shoulder — or maybe I'd be reclining on the rocks of a secret cove while a boy windsurfed in the photo's middle distance. Look further, below the surface, Skye's voice intruded into my mind. Okay, so the photos wouldn't show that the horse was dribbling green foam onto my clean shirt, or that the rocks in the cove were poking into my back. Were things like that happening in the photographs of my mother? Was my album full of unseen pains and irritations?

I sighed. The surface of things was so much easier to arrange.

When I reached Rose Mullion, there was no answer to my knock at the door. I wandered around to the garden but no one was in sight. As I descended the terraces, I became aware of voices in the thick shrubbery. I paused.

"When? Soon?" asked a harsh voice with a foreign accent. A woman's voice.

"I don't know yet. Be patient," answered Richard, sounding impatient.

"Soon?" persisted the woman. "Is not safe for me. Is danger."

"Can't help it. I'm busy this week, big races," snapped Richard. "I'll talk to my contact. To Jean Paul."

Yikes. I realized with a sudden guilty start that I was eavesdropping. How to let them know I was here? I began whistling. "Blondie!" I called.

The dog didn't appear, but Richard rushed out from behind the bushes, scowling fiercely. When he saw me, he rearranged his face. All the downward shooting lines in his lean cheeks turned around and creased upward as he grinned. How could he look so different so quickly? I stared at him in fascination. Feelings couldn't change that fast under the surface of a face, could they?

"Ah, Stella, nice to see you," he said. "Nicholas is down in the cove. I've got to run. There's a big race out of Falmouth this week and my yacht's entered. I've got to get things shipshape."

At the bottom of the garden, I paused and looked back. Richard had disappeared, but the dowdy woman in the head scarf was kneeling by one of the terrace walls, pulling weeds from around yellow stonecrop flowers. There was something different about her clothes; she didn't look as if she belonged here. Who was she? I sensed there was some secret about her, some mystery. What country was she from and why was she here? What did Richard mean about a contact? Why did the woman feel she was in danger?

As though sensing my stare, she swiveled around and stared down the garden at me with her dark, deep sunk eyes. Her face creased with anxiety. She didn't wave or speak, and after a minute she bent over her weeding again and I scrambled down the path to the cove.

Blondie loped to meet me at the bottom. "You're pleased to see me anyway," I crooned, stroking her elegant muzzle as her feathery tail swept the air. Now to find Nicholas. I crossed the beach and peered into the boathouse, then noticed that the white yacht was gone from the cove and the zodiac was missing from the slipway. Maybe I was on my own. I decided to explore the rock pools again. I left my straw bag, containing my birthday snorkel and mask, a *J-17* magazine, my disc player and two CDs, sitting on the hull of a small sailing boat. With a towel over my arm and my wallet in a tiny white shoulder bag, I headed across to the rocks and scrambled up their barnacle-crusted ridges.

"Oh, hi!" I said. "I didn't know you were here."

Nicholas nodded. "Hello," he replied, without taking his headphones off. He was propped against a hot rock with a towel behind his back, and was wearing nothing but baggy blue shorts. A sketchpad was open on his knees and he held a pencil loosely in one hand.

I tried not to stare at his long legs, stretched out at eye level. I got busy hauling myself up the rock and explained, "Your dad invited me to lunch."

"Cool." His toes waved to a rhythm that only he could hear.

I dropped my towel beside him and bent to unlace my sandals. At home, when we'd turned twelve, Noah had suddenly learned to say "cool" like a flat line, the sound a dead person's body makes on a hospital monitor. No emotion escaped from his mouth when he said that word. But I always knew what he really meant. Nicholas said "cool" the same way, but I couldn't read his mind. Did his "cool" mean that he was happy I'd come for lunch or that he couldn't care less? Did it mean "let's be friends" or "buzz off and leave me alone"? What lay behind the flat, hard surface of that word? I decided to try another topic.

"Where's the boat gone?" I asked, gesturing to the empty bay where the green swell lifted dark banks of golden kelp.

"Moored in Falmouth," Nicholas replied. I shot him a quick glance. He wasn't smiling and I couldn't tell what his eyes might be doing behind his dark shades.

"Are you crewing?" I asked.

"Maybe."

Perhaps a third topic might do the trick; they say, "third time lucky." "What are you sketching?" I asked, trying to sound casual. He must have noticed my eyes sliding toward his pad, because he flipped its green covers shut.

"Nothing much," he replied.

Okay, Mr. Joe Cool, I thought, I can take a hint.

Enough questions already. Sorry I asked. Balancing between the pointed cones of limpet shells and the sharp ridges of barnacles, I picked my way over the rocks with my back to Nicholas. Was he watching me go? I tried to move like a model, gliding over the barnacles with smooth, floating gestures.

Ouch! Aargh! Oww!

I stumbled over a crack, holding up my stubbed toe and hopping inelegantly on one foot.

My arms spun like windmill sails. Pay attention to the terrain, I scolded myself. The difference between a runway's flat surface and the craggy Cornish rocks was quite noticeable if you were in a noticing frame of mind. My toe was definitely noticing, throbbing like a drumbeat, but the wound seemed superficial. No dripping blood. Maybe blood would be good; maybe it would stir some protective I'll-look-after-you-now sort of instinct in Nicholas. How old did boys have to be to develop this instinct? Did it arrive on a certain birthday, like the way they knew how to say "cool" when they turned twelve?

The first pool I found was shallow, its warm water home to a tiny darting fish. The second pool was closer to the edge of the sea. Every few minutes, a wave would trickle in over the rim of the pool and send ripples flooding across my reflection. Green and golden weed stirred in the ripples. The sea was like a living creature, an animal breathing in a long, slow rhythm, glopping and sucking at the hot rocks. I wished Noah was with me; we could have shared the pools, the empty shells I stuffed into one pocket. Our friendly shadows would have leaped over the rocks together.

I glanced back at Nicholas. His toes were still keeping time with the beat, and he was spreading sunscreen over his bronze arms.

"Do you think it's time for lunch?" I called.

"Dunno." He sounded bored by the idea of food.

I scrambled over hot rocks to the next pool and squatted down to study it. Clusters of red anemones, like exotic flowers, waved their tentacles along the bottom. I plunged my arm in to pull out a white shell wedged in a crack. The water was freezing cold, numbing my fingers. I climbed on to the next pool. When I finally looked back, Nicholas was standing up and folding his towel. I shaded my eyes and watched his wiry silhouette against the glittering sea.

"Tide!" he shouted to me, and began to climb off the rocks. I noticed how small the beach had become, how the foamy waves were sluicing far up the sand. I scrambled after Nicholas and ran across the grating shingle, catching up to him near the smugglers' rock cut.

"Does the whole beach disappear at high tide?" I panted.

"Nope." His back was turned to me already as he climbed up the cut. If I don't follow, I thought, he'll just keep going to the top without me. I ran a sticky hand over my forehead, lifting my bangs. My head ached with the heat, my toes pulsed with pain, and my stomach growled hungrily.

Suddenly, anger flared in me like lightening, violent and unexpected. I scrambled up the rock cut after Nicholas. "What's your problem?" I hissed at him.

"What?"

"Can't you just — act like a human being?" I asked, waving my arms. "You think you're Daddy Cool or something? You can't talk to me? I'm not good enough for you?"

His shades stared blankly at me; all I could see was my own tiny face, a distorted reflection. Maybe that was how I looked when I was mad; I could imagine anger pulling my face around like silly putty.

"Well, answer me!" I spluttered into his silence.

"I didn't invite you here," he said with a shrug of his shoulders.

"Fine. I'll leave! Some people enjoy my company! I'll take the bus. Fine!"

I yanked my sandals on, jerked the laces tight, and flung myself up the path. My lips were pressed together to hold in my panting. Gravel spurted from under my feet and rolled down the cliff. Was Nicholas following me? From the corner of the house, I sneaked a quick glance over my shoulder. He was standing under a palm tree at the top of the garden, watching me. Was it just my imagination — or did he look miserable? His shoulders seemed to be slumped at dejected angles. Before he could do or say anything (like that was a possibility), I strode around the corner of the house and down the lane.

At the road, I found a granite stile where a little green lizard was soaking up the sun. It flicked its tail and ran off when my shadow arrived. I perched on the stone and settled in to wait for a bus, my jaw set at a determined angle. I could wait all afternoon if that's what it took. I'd show him, I thought.

Under the surface of my anger I was slightly confused

about *what* I was showing him, but I ignored this confusion. It had to be temporary, right? Like when the computer forgets for half an hour how to format paragraphs. Take a break and *voila!* the problem vanishes. One of these days, any moment now, my mind will function with utmost clarity. I'll know the answer to any question the world poses.

In the meantime, I'd be happy to recognize the sound of a bus engine lurching around bends.

CHAPTER SEVEN

Dear Dad, thanks for the money for the helicopter trip to the Scilly Isles. As you can see from this postcard, we made it. The islands are twenty-seven miles off Land's End — specks of rock and white sand. There's a myth that Atlantis used to lie in between. The stories call it Lyonesse. We jigged for mackerel today — I caught some! Wish you and Noah were here. How's your leg?

Love Stella

It began to spit rain as I trudged up the street beside Skye, feeling frazzled. The straps of my backpack rubbed on my bare, sunburned shoulders and my hair was wiry with salt. The helicopter had brought us as far as Penzance, on the Cornish mainland, and then we'd caught a train to Truro and another train to Falmouth. We'd only been away for three days but somehow it felt longer; the Scilly Isles seemed like a time-warp place, a landscape where the century moved forward at a different speed. Skye had heard the islands were an inspiring place for artists, and I hoped she'd got inspiration because what I'd got were blisters. At least the trip had given me something else to think about. We'd flown two days after my fight with Nicholas and I'd been happy to leave his part of the world even briefly. And I'd written four new poems in the time that Skye had spent washing quick watercolor sketches into her pad.

The sun had shone while we were away, but now gray clouds scudded over the palm trees in a rising wind.

"We're just going to make it home in time," said Skye, and she was right.

As I dumped my pack onto the sofa, rain began to pelt down hard, stippling the surface of the harbor. From the window, I watched anchored boats toss uneasily and ferries throw waves of white spray that the wind carried sideways.

Skye was in the galley-style kitchen, rummaging in the fridge. "There's enough leftovers here for Bubble and Squeak," she informed me.

"For what?"

"That's English for leftovers fried up," she said with a laugh.

It didn't sound to me like a laughing matter; right

then, I could have gone for pizza in a big way. Bubble
and Squeak sounded even worse than tzatziki or tahini
or any of the other things Skye made.

"I'm not too hungry right now," I said, then headed
for a hot soak in the tub before my rumbling stomach
could tell Skye the truth. When I came out half an hour
later, Skye was sitting in the middle of the front room
doing her yoga thing.

"Your supper's in the oven," she said.

I cracked the door open. Rats. Supper still looked like
leftovers and not pizza. I couldn't watch TV, since Skye
had to have "calm" to do her yoga, so the leftovers and
I headed for my room. I pulled the chair that was usually
by the dresser over to the window and sat by the floral
curtains to eat. Rain streamed down the windowpane,
and the water in the harbor heaved with waves. Below
the apartments, waves hit the wall with a smack and
shot messily into the air.

What this gourmet meal and idyllic setting lacked was
a little music. I hunted around for my CD player but it
wasn't in any of the usual places. I looked on the table
by my bed but only the framed picture of my mother,
holding me in her arms, sat there. I never went anywhere
without this picture. In it, I was about two, a chubby-
cheeked infant. My mother and I were both looking into
the light; our onion-skin hair tossed by wind. For the
millionth time, I noticed how our eyes were the same
shape when we smiled. Then I gave myself a shake and
went on searching for my CD player.

I peered under the bed. Not there. And there was
nothing in the top drawer of the dresser except under-

wear. I opened other drawers, then glanced at the windowsill. The CD player was in none of these places. I frowned. Had I taken it to the Scilly Isles? Suddenly, I had a horrible image of exactly where it was, along with two CDs, a *J-17* magazine, my snorkel and mask, and my new straw bag. They were all lying on the hull of a sailing dinghy, inside the boathouse in the cove at Rose Mullion. I'd been so mad after the confrontation with Nicholas that I'd stormed away without them.

This was majorly bad news. I glowered out my window at the tossing harbor. I'd have to catch the bus to Rose Mullion tomorrow and sneak down to the cove to retrieve my possessions. In the meantime, would the rain be blowing into the boathouse and getting my stuff wet? Or would the stormy waves sluice under the boat hulls, jiggling my stuff loose, tipping it into the salt water? Would I have to face Nicholas one last time?

"Come and see this!" called Skye's voice, muffled by my closed door. I sighed theatrically. Sometimes life doesn't know when to leave a person alone with her problems.

"What?" I asked, trudging into the front room.

Skye gestured to the TV, which she'd turned on after finishing her yoga. The screen was filled with an aerial view of islands ringed by white beaches. The Scillies?

". . . long known for their tropical gardens," the narrator's voice was saying. "After this break, we will return to *Lost and Golden Places* and learn more about Atlantis and other legends."

"They're going to talk about where we've just been," Skye explained. "I thought you might be interested."

"Cool," I said — a flat-line sound — even though I was kind of interested. I'd decided to act around Skye the way I did around phys. ed. teachers at school: cooperative but not too lively. Any encouragement and they got totally carried away about things. I plopped onto the paint sheet covering the sofa and picked at my supper while the commercials did a silent sales pitch. Skye always turned the sound off. She said all the asinine noise cluttered up her mind.

Actually, supper wasn't as bad as I'd feared (fried potatoes and onions and bits of sausage and some kind of green leafy vegetable) but, in keeping with my unenthusiastic thing, I didn't make any appreciative noises. This approach was my Survival Strategy; I figured I needed one if Skye and I had to get along for another three weeks.

The commercial break ended and Skye turned on the TV volume: a sudden surge of violin music accompanied a computer-animated graphic of a massive, aqua-green wave. The wave crest curled over, hung suspended, then crashed down on the roofs of churches and cottages.

"Not a toothpaste ad," I observed. "This stuff gets rid of more than plaque."

"Shhh."

The announcer decided to join our conversation. "Is this how Atlantis ended, in a catastrophic moment?" he debated portentously. "In Cornwall the fate of Lyonesse, the lost land, is recorded in several collections of mythology. Only one man, called Trevanion, is purported to have escaped the inrushing water, riding a white horse. Other sources cite the Mediterranean as the location of

Atlantis, a land that disappeared when tectonic and volcanic forces wrenched the known world apart and let the waters of the Atlantic pour in, creating the Mediterranean Sea."

More graphics of huge waves, tolling bells in crumbling church towers, people being swept away over inundated fields. Just the right kind of program for a stormy, wet evening.

Skye blew thoughtfully onto her green tea and threw me a blanket when she noticed me rubbing at goose bumps on my legs. It was almost dark already.

The violins sang toward a crescendo. "While the truth may never be fully uncovered," the narrator stated, "certain facts remain constant. Humans have, and always will, devote time and effort in search of things lost — compelled perhaps by the mystery inherent in their loss."

"Humph," muttered Skye, turning off the sound again as a commercial for a super-size, hovering chocolate bar flickered on. "In other words, people don't know when to let things go. There are things in life to hold onto, and other things to let go of. An important difference."

After the hovering chocolate, a car that was guaranteed to get your husband/wife/kids safely home, a cell phone even a dog could use, and two commercials for pop, the documentary resumed. This time, the topic was El Dorado, the mythical city that the Spanish conquistadors spent their lives searching for, the city paved with gold. Soldiers in iron hats, horses, lines of slaves. Hot sun. Fever. Misery in the jungle. Death far from home. The violins sobbed while the narrator summed things up with another pithy observation: "Man's restless soul

impels him to engage in mystical journeys toward the
unattainable, the vision of perfection."

"Humph," said Skye again. "Another way of saying
we're too stupid to know what we need out of life."

"But maybe the conquistadors really believed in El
Dorado," I said. "If you really believed in something,
wouldn't you try to find it?"

Skye stared at me thoughtfully for a moment. "What
I think is, we all get 'hooked' by some vision of life, some
dream. However, there are attainable dreams and unattainable ones. So before you get sucked into spending
your life pursuing something, you want to make sure it's
something you can find. Something real and worth finding. Worth pursuing."

"Like what are you meaning?"

She paused again, glancing around the dim room. Her
gaze landed on one of my magazines and she fanned the
pages at me. "Like this," she said. "Visions of impossible beauty. Unattainable stuff. Hair, clothes, bodies that
most women will never have but will spend their lives
trying to get. Their own personal El Dorado."

See what happened when I broke the rules of my not-
getting-involved Survival Strategy? I glared at Skye.

"You wouldn't look so bad yourself if you bothered
with some basics," I said insultingly. "And if you had
any kids, you'd know that we don't like being lectured."

My words vibrated in the air, like sounds from plucked
guitar strings.

I'd gone too far. Way too far. Dad's admonition about
not giving Skye hassle was down over the horizon somewhere. Skye's expression was one I'd never seen on her

face before; her nostrils were pinched and white and there was a steely glint in her eyes.

"Stella," she said in a voice leveled at me like a pointing finger, "if you'd ever bothered to get to know me, you'd have found that I am a real person behind my untidy hair and my stocky body and all the other things you see when you look at me. The reason I don't have children is that I became pregnant when my husband and I were studying at a remote ashram in India. There were complications in my fifth month; by the time we got out of the mountains to a hospital, I lost my baby. A girl. Due to an infection, I could never have another baby. Two years later, my husband left me. So, unfortunately for you, I haven't had the chance to learn how to talk to surly teenagers."

Sometimes silence is louder than the loudest noise. That's how it was in the room right then: a roaring silence battered against me. I huddled down small on the sofa, shrinking inside my skin. I wanted to shrink so small that Skye wouldn't be able to see me. I wanted to shrink so small that I would cease to exist, would never have to use my voice again. Do you know that emotions have temperatures? Shame feels like lava in your veins.

"I wasn't intending to lecture you," Skye said at last. Her voice sounded heavy and tired. Her words seemed to travel a long way to reach me, through thick air, like light from a star. "Sometimes I'm just thinking out loud, Stella. The death of my baby was something I've had to learn to let go of, and having a family of my own is something I've had to stop traveling toward. I've had to admit it's a golden city I will never reach."

Rain hit the window with a hard spatter and the tiny me inside my huge skin jumped like a bug in a sack. When I swallowed, my throat seemed impossibly long.

"Sorry, Skye. I'm sorry," I muttered, and then I fled on a surge of misery, closed the door to my room, and lay face down on my bed listening to the wind.

All night the wind moaned and wailed against the old warehouse, waking me from a fitful sleep. I imagined the water in the harbor gathering itself into one huge wave that would hang suspended over the town of Falmouth, then crash down and obliterate everything. It would be even bigger than my shame. Sometimes, over the sound of wind and rain and crashing water, I heard a sharp, shattering sound like something breaking. In the morning, looking down, I saw that the parking lot by the harbor was strewn with broken slates, the stone that the roof tiles in Cornwall are made of. The wind had blown them down. The harbor was churned up with whitecaps, and low clouds scudded across the sky.

I lurked in my room, reading a book or staring out at the storm. My CD player was probably ruined, I thought. The sea would have washed it from the boathouse. It was too stormy to take the bus to Rose Mullion today.

When I tiptoed out on a food run, Skye was painting at a new canvas, the largest one I'd seen her use yet. "Morning, Stella," she said. Her voice was friendly, but she didn't turn around from her work. I glimpsed splotches of cobalt and cream, gray and aqua on the canvas. The colors of the Scilly Isles. Was she thinking about her own lost lands as she smeared the colors on?

Later, she came to my closed door and called my

name. "I'm going to my art class," she said. "I don't think it will be canceled. If you go out, stay away from the water. There's bread and sandwich stuff for lunch."

"Yes," I replied. "Okay. Thanks."

Homesickness hurt in my stomach. I wished I could lounge on a sofa with Noah, feeling the familiar hard bones of his shoulder against mine, sharing a bag of chips, reading his thoughts. However, I had to admit that some kind of new reality was emerging in my relationship with Noah. We didn't seem to do so many things together anymore: we didn't jump off the barn beams into the hay; we didn't build forts in the fields. I wondered whether Noah noticed how we were turning into a male and a female, falling into roles. While I read fashion magazines, he played video games; while I listened to boyband CDs, he made the basketball team. When we were little kids, our bodies were almost identical: skinny arms, straight backs; even our short, shaggy haircuts were similar. And our piping voices used to confuse people: who was speaking? But now Noah's voice seemed to vibrate in his ribs, and his hair was buzzed short, and I had breasts.

Lying in my Cornish room, far away from Noah, I tried to figure out if these things mattered. In some ways they did, because thinking about them made me feel sad. But in other ways, I knew they didn't matter. Noah was still the person who could read my thoughts. Did he know how miserable I was feeling right now? Did a frown ghost across his face as he dipped a canoe paddle into the water? Did the wind in the pine trees sigh my name in his ears?

And what about Dad, home alone in a cast? I wished
I could hug him, bury my nose in his soft cotton shirt,
and hear his voice say my name. Did he miss me . . . did
he miss Skye? Did it bother him that I couldn't like Skye?
Did he hope this trip would change things? Oh, life was
too complicated!

I wanted to lay my cheek against Malibu's long face
and breathe in his comforting, horsy smell. I wanted a
plate of Pearl's macaroni and cheese.

If only I'd had room in my luggage for the photo
albums with the pictures of my mother. If only she were
here, to warm me with a smile. I thought about how
there was not a single picture of her looking sad, angry,
anxious, hopeful, confused, thoughtful, tired, lonely,
sad, jealous, concerned. In all the pictures, she was smiling and happy — gorgeous and happy. But no one was
like that all the time. Was my mother just a myth, like
Atlantis and El Dorado, existing only in the imagination? Was the mystery of her loss all that I had left of her
to hold onto? Was the thought of being gorgeous all that
I had to travel toward, to set my compass by?

I cried into tissue after tissue, filling the wicker waste-
basket with crumpled, soggy balls. Homesickness ached
in my bones, made me cold. I dragged on the warmest
sweater I'd brought with me, and a pair of jeans, and
borrowed Skye's thick, wooly socks for my feet. I opened
the book in which I wrote my poems and read through
them all, but when I tried to write a new one, my feelings wouldn't translate with any rhythm or grace. My
words were like rocks on the page: clunky and hard.

From between the pages of my journal, where I'd

placed it for safekeeping on this trip, I pulled out the letter my mother had written to me before she died. Even
though I knew it by heart, I read it again. She'd printed
it because I was only six and learning to read at the time.
Her letters looked as wavering and unformed as my own
had on the blue lines of school paper.

It was a short note. It told me how much she loved
me, that I was her star. It told me to always be friends
with my brother and that my father was a good man
who would take care of me and love me always. It
thanked me for my poems and pictures, the ones I'd
brought to the hospital. It reminded me that after the
rain there would be a rainbow. I mean, there isn't a lot
one can write to a six-year-old daughter when one is
dying, right? Although there weren't any big answers for
me in this note, I took it everywhere I went and treasured
it more than any other possession.

But there was one line at the end that always puzzled
me, that sounded as though my mother had started talking to the older person I'd turn into, the one she wouldn't
be around to know. *A mother's wish is that her children
don't repeat her mistakes*, she'd written. I had stared at
those words a thousand times but I still didn't know
what they meant. It was as though my mother had
started thinking onto the page. But what mistakes was
she referring to? How could I avoid them if I didn't
know?

Once, when I was about ten, I'd asked my dad what
mistakes my mother had made. He'd given me a long
look, but as if he was looking through me instead of at
me, and he'd sighed and said it was not people's mistakes

that were important but what they did to fix them. Then he asked me if I wanted spaghetti for lunch.

Finally the rain eased. I refolded the note from my mother and put it away safely. I decided to go out for a walk. The northeast wind funneled down the narrow streets of town, and wet cobbles shone with a dull gleam. The streets were almost empty; only a few stubborn people struggled with umbrellas that kept flipping inside out. A Coastguard Search and Rescue helicopter whirred over, battling the wind as it headed toward the sea, its red-and-white paint bright against the dark sky. The fronds on palm trees clattered noisily together, and when I walked near the water I saw a small boat that had broken from its moorings and was being battered against the harbor wall by the waves. Once, a falling slate shattered just behind me. I almost wished it had hit me. I felt like I deserved some kind of punishment. I snugged my chin into my collar, and bent my head against the wind.

I felt like I'd come to the end of something; I was numb inside as well as out. Confusion tangled my thoughts. All I could focus on was going to Rose Mullion after the storm and rescuing my things out of the boathouse. It seemed important to have all the bits of myself to take back to Canada and the people who loved me.

It was going to take all my strength to hold every bit in place until I got to safety.

CHAPTER EIGHT

When I walked down to Rose Mullion the day after the storm, the house was silent, its windows blank and dark. In one window, I glimpsed Blondie looking out at me. In the garden, the plumes on the pampas grass had been shredded by the gale. Palm leaves and broken branches were strewn haphazardly across the wet grass.

I reached the cliff path without seeing anyone. The wind had swung into the southwest and felt warm and boisterous against me, like an energetic dog. It flapped the corners of my windbreaker and flung my hair around. Below me, the sea churned dramatically against the headlands, gray-green waves sending up gouts of water. The path was slippery with rain. I climbed down carefully, glad I'd worn my hiking boots.

In the cove, hungry waves rushed at my feet then dragged shingle back into the sea with a grating roar that filled my head. Movement caught my eye and I glanced toward the rocks. Nicholas was balanced on a boulder with his back to me; he seemed to be watching the waves crashing in. I held my breath, willing him not to look around and see me. Suddenly he jumped out of sight, going around the corner of the headland into the next cove. If I was quick I could leave before he returned.

I reached the boathouse and peered in. The two dinghies had been dragged as far inside as possible. There was nothing on them except unstepped masts: no straw bag, no CDs or player, no magazine, no snorkel and mask. I peered at the wet sand under the hulls. Nothing. I craned my neck to where sails were draped over the rafters. Nothing. It was what I'd expected but now that it had actually happened I couldn't believe it. I wanted my stuff. Tears prickled behind my eyes.

"Peachy marvelous, baby," I said to myself bitterly. This was Ashley's phrase, but she always said it like a joke and we always laughed.

I began to trudge back across the beach, feeling like I might never laugh again, not caring when a wave poured across my feet and soaked cold into my socks.

"Stella! Stella!"

I paused and looked back. Oh, joy. Nicholas had returned. He was balanced on the rocks again, waving his arms. Through my dismal gloom, it took me a moment to notice his face. It was alive with some kind of crackling energy — excitement maybe? What was going on? I stared as though I'd never seen him before.

"Stella. Come here!" he yelled, his words tattered by the wind.

Was this a trick of some kind? Was something wrong? I stared at him for a moment longer, just so he wouldn't think he could say "Jump," and I'd reply, "How high?" Then curiosity got the better of me and I trudged back across the shingle, not hurrying. I didn't look at him again until I'd climbed onto the rocks beside him. That was when things got really weird.

First of all, he smiled at me. I almost looked over my shoulder to see who was standing there. His smile changed his whole face; his skin sort of shone over his cheekbones and the sharp angle of his jaw. His blue eyes sparkled. The next thing that happened was even more totally amazing — he grabbed my arm, a friendly kind of grabbing like Noah did when he wanted to share something.

"What?" I asked suspiciously.

"I've found a baby seal in the next cove!" he said breathlessly. "I think we'll have to rescue it!"

"You're kidding?" But I knew he wasn't. Excitement tingled out of his warm grip and into my arm. "Come on!" I yelled. "Let's go!"

We leaped across the rocks, the treads on my hikers rasping on rough granite and barnacles. We were like two deer, bounding over crevices where black water gurgled ominously, jumping across rock pools full of flying clouds. Around the headland, Nicholas jumped down

onto another beach and I landed just behind him,
breathing hard.

"Look!"

I followed the line of his arm. This beach was similar
to the one in Rose Mullion's cove: dark wet sand, banks
of gray shingle, and tangled masses of weed and rope
flung up by the storm. At the far end of the beach, at the
edge of the frothy water, lay a pale furry lump about
three feet long. Nicholas and I sprinted toward it, then
slowed down for the last bit and crept up slowly. The
baby seal's eyes were dark brown and big and round.
Puppy eyes.

"He's crying," I said, nearly starting to cry myself. I
knelt on the wet sand beside him, and he flopped awkwardly sideways to get away. After a moment, he gave
up and lay still, as if too tired to bother moving.

"Careful," warned Nicholas as the pup opened a wide,
bright-pink mouth. "He's got teeth, he might bite."

"Where's his mother?"

"Not around. Maybe she got separated from him in
the storm. He's very little."

We stared at the pup's bedraggled white coat. A cut
near his right eye seeped blood.

"Look at his flipper," I said. One toe was almost torn
off, and blood trickled into the sand.

"He's been battered against the rocks," guessed
Nicholas. "We have to call the Seal Sanctuary. They have
a Landrover and a rescue team for seals."

"Where are they?"

"At Gweek, over on the Lizard Peninsula, but they'll
come anywhere. You run back to the house and tele-

phone. I'll stay here and make sure nothing happens to the seal."

I hesitated; I didn't want to leave the pup and his sad brown eyes. I wanted to wrap him up in a hug and make him safe. I remembered a canoeing trip with Dad, when Noah and I were nine. We'd tipped the canoe and got soaked, cold to the marrow. Dad had wrapped us in blankets. "The main thing is to keep warm," his voice said now in my head. Did seals get cold?

"Go on," urged Nicholas. "The tide turned ages ago. It must be halfway in already."

"We should wrap the pup up," I said, "to keep him warm. And you might have to move him higher up the beach, away from the tide. He's too wet and slippery to hold. We need to wrap him up."

We stared around, as if a blanket might fall from the sky. Then I looked at Nicholas but he was only wearing shorts and a long sleeved T-shirt. Slowly I pulled my windbreaker off, then shrugged my sweater over my head.

"Your pullover?" asked Nicholas doubtfully. "Are you sure?"

"Yes," I said firmly, and felt only a tiny pang as I draped my very best, very favorite, very expensive mohair and lambswool sweater over the seal's wet back.

"See you soon!" I said, turning into the wind.

"Tell them Poldhu Cove, east of Mullion Head!" Nicholas instructed me.

I struggled across the slippery beach. At the rocks, I took one glance back; Nicholas was huddled down by the seal, looking as though he was talking to it. I leaped

over the rocks, jogged across the cove, panted up the cliff
path. By the time I reached Rose Mullion, my lungs felt
ready to burst.

I hammered on the door but there was no answer, and
after a brief wait I simply went in. My boots left wet
tread marks on the slate kitchen floor. I remembered that
there was a telephone by the fridge, and I fumbled
through the directory that I found on a chair nearby. The
newsprint pages clung to my damp, shaking fingers.
Finally I just punched in zero and told the operator what
I wanted; maybe she detected the urgency in my tone
because she put me through right away.

"Gweek Seal Sanctuary," said a male voice.

"I'm calling from Rose Mullion, a house. There's a
baby seal on the beach with no mother. It needs help!" I
rattled off.

The other voice remained calm. I gave directions as
best I could; he said the rescue team was already out
near Falmouth and could reach Rose Mullion quickly.

When I hung up, my legs started shaking. Should I
wait for the team to arrive or go back to Nicholas? I was
too excited to hang around so I decided to run back and
check on things, then return in time to meet the seal's
rescuers.

Halfway down the cliff path, I froze. The rising tide
was sending huge rollers, smooth as oil, into the cove.
They smashed on the rocks, breaking into towers of
spray. The wind carried their salty mist into my face,
coating my lips. The beach was only a thin strip, and
waves rushed up it toward the weed heaped along the
high tide line. We were running out of time — the tide

might beat us. Then what would happen to the little seal? I couldn't bear the thought of abandoning him back to the harsh sea and the cruel rocks, when he'd come so close to being saved.

I doubled my fists and sprinted, gasping, across the shingle. I struggled over the rocks. A wave, surging under them in a hidden channel, exploded upward through a crack and drenched my legs. I swallowed a yell of pure terror. Rock pools were swelling before my eyes, filling with cold sea.

"Nicholas!" I yelled, even before I'd climbed over the highest rocks and could see him. He was five yards away, also up on the rocks. The seal was in his arms, completely wrapped in my best mohair sweater. Even its face was wrapped, maybe so it couldn't bite.

Between Nicholas and me, a tongue of boiling water surged through a narrow channel in the rocks.

"It's the zawn!" Nicholas yelled, gesturing at the channel. "I can't cross it! It's too deep now."

For one wild moment I stared at him, trying to understand what he meant. But part of me knew immediately. Nicholas was trapped by the tide. Since I had jumped across, hardly noticing it, the zawn had doubled in width. Golden weed lashed in its black, rolling waters.

I pointed toward the base of the cliff, where the zawn ended in a chaos of steep, jumbled rock. "You could climb there!" I shouted.

"I can't climb with the seal! Stella, go back!"

"I can't leave you!" I shouted in panic.

"Go and call the Coast Guard. Dial 999. They'll have to take me up the cliff!"

I stared at the wall of rock behind him, foot after towering foot of granite, seamed with ledges where wildflowers shook in the wind.

"Go on!" he yelled. "Hurry!"

Was he scared? His eyes met mine with a steady, level gaze. I knew this was an image I'd always carry around: the courageous, determined angle of his jaw; his wiry arms wrapped around the seal; his hair feathered by wind.

I spun away. Rocks blurred beneath me. I didn't even think about where to place my feet, where to land when I jumped off boulders. My body took over as adrenaline coursed through me, making me invincible, an athlete for half an hour. Dimly, I felt pride in my body, the agile strength of my muscles. All those hours of pounding around the school track, and flinging myself at high jumps and long jumps, seemed suddenly worthwhile.

When I reached the kitchen of Rose Mullion, I punched in 999 but could hardly speak. "Help!" I babbled, my lungs burning. "Someone's trapped by the tide!" Again, I explained the beach's location to a calm male voice.

"Come quickly!" I begged; right then, I would have got down on my knees, I would have crawled — done anything that would've helped speed up the rescue services.

As I staggered outside, a cream-colored Land Rover came up the lane and stopped by the house. S.O.S. was painted in green on the door panel. Two women in overalls jumped out and waved. Their cheeks were red with wind, their hair pulled into ponytails.

"Hello! I'm Marie and this is Jeannie. Where's the seal?" one of them asked.

I pointed eastward, past the slight roll in the land that marked the shoulder of Mullion Head. "In Poldhu Cove!" I said. "But it's too late! My friend's trapped and I've called the Coast Guard."

The women exchanged worried frowns; then the one called Jeannie laid a reassuring arm along my shoulder. I was twitchy with panic.

"It's alright," she said soothingly. "We'll go and take a look with the Landrover. Hop in."

There were only two seats in the cab, which was filled with a stench of fish and wet rubber. I shared the passenger seat with Marie. We bounced through a field, opening and closing gates while cows watched us with mildeyed curiosity. Then we were on the exposed cliff top, swaying across the headland on a rough track, furze clawing at the tires.

The journey took forever.

Come on, I thought. Please hurry. But I knew we couldn't go any faster on the uneven ground. Outcroppings of granite tipped the Landrover from side to side. Was Nicholas still there? I squeezed my eyes tightly against the thought of him being sucked into the sea, into its whirlpools, its cold currents where the skulls of drowned sailors drifted like lost planets.

Above the cove, we jumped out and crept carefully to the edge of the cliff. I peered down.

Dizzying, cold space.

Rocks. A tiny strip of shingle. Foamy white waves.

My heart clenched like a fist. My eyes ached. "Nicholas!" I screamed into the wind. "Nicholas!"

Nothing. Wind ringing in my ears.

Then Nicholas' small figure stepped out from the base of the cliff and his face tilted upward. He couldn't wave; he was still holding the bundled seal. A sob of relief jumped from my mouth, and Marie laid a hand on my arm. "He's okay at the base of the cliff for now," she said. "The tide won't reach him there for a while."

Was she telling me the truth? I had no way of knowing. The sea, I understood now, was not like the lakes at home. In the spring, when the snow melted in Ontario, the rivers ran wild and the lakes crept high up their banks. For a few weeks we avoided the water, but then the level would drop and the rivers would move calmly and slowly on their limestone beds. The lakes grew warm and placid, soupy with water lilies and duckweeds.

But the sea was different — an animal that could grow hungry whenever it chose. Staring down at Nicholas far below, I saw how the sea rushed hungrily in toward the cliff to chew its rocky crust. I saw how it would lick Nicholas into its dark stomach with one swift swipe of its powerful tongue; how it was a force no one could survive. It flooded rock pools, mauled boulders. It rushed and slithered, all muscle and power.

"We have to do something!" I shrieked at the seal women, my voice cracking with fear. Jeannie pointed and I turned to look. Along the rough track, two vehicles were approaching: a dark blue truck and a dark blue Landrover with a yellow roof. On both vehicles, H.M. Coastguard blazed brilliant red. The trucks growled up to us; four men in bright blue jumpsuits swarmed onto the cliff top.

"Down there!" I shouted, pointing.

The men looked over the cliff, their faces stern and calm but not alarmed.

"You have to help him!" I shouted. "And he has a seal!"

"A seal?"

They held a quick conference, huddled against the wind. Auxiliary Coastguard, I read on the shoulders of their jumpsuits, as I strained to catch their words.

"The Scotsman?"

"Yes. Jim'll go down. The boy first, then the seal."

"Righto."

I watched as they hauled equipment from the Landrover: ropes and stakes, metal bars, a portable red engine. I didn't see how this stuff could help. I jigged anxiously from foot to foot on purple heather flowers. Marie hauled an empty wire crate from the back of the Sanctuary Landrover. As I peered over her shoulder, I saw there was another crate in the back, with a seal already in it. It had been there all the time I'd been bumping over the headland in the passenger seat. Fish breath, I thought.

The coastguards were hammering a metal stake into the ground, back from the edge of the cliff. One of them started the engine; another was knotting and coiling ropes. The third man passed ropes from the metal stake over a tripod standing near the cliff's edge. Then suddenly the man called Jim picked up a handle attached to a set of double ropes and walked backward off the cliff.

My breath stopped in my throat.

The crate for the seal was roped to him, making him dangerously off balance. He hung suspended in the turbulent air, rocking on his pair of ropes that stretched back to the engine. Slowly he went down the cliff, toward the sharp rocks and tumbling sea. Once, rocks fell from under his boots and Nicholas ducked out of sight.

At the top of the cliff, no one spoke. A radio crackled in the Coastguard truck, and a seagull cried mournfully.

I wondered if the ropes ever broke. One of the auxiliaries seemed to read my thoughts. "Tough nylon rope," he said with a reassuring nod. "This metal bar we put here on the edge of the cliff — see? — stops the rope from chafing on the rocks."

I nodded and peered over again, fighting vertigo.

The man had reached the bottom and was on the rocks. He was talking to Nicholas — explaining things? He untied the ropes around the crate and flipped the lid open. Nicholas bent over, laying the seal in the crate, which Jim then roped shut again. He carried the crate out of sight, closer to the base of the cliff.

Slowly, he started up the cliff with Nicholas beside him, while the portable engine ran with a steady, hard beat, turning the wheel and pulling the ropes upward. At first the two figures didn't seem to get any bigger, then suddenly they were just below us. Nicholas was hauled onto the heather by strong arms. Relief rushed through me and I flung my arms around him, burying my face in the cold, rumpled folds of his T-shirt. A ragged cheer went up from the seal women and the auxiliaries.

I backed off, looking away.

Silence fell again as Jim went back over the cliff. Time crawled. Nicholas breathed beside me in short bursts. We still didn't look at each other. Instead we watched Jim making the journey back up the cliff with the seal in its crate. His face, as it rose over the lip of the cliff, was wet with sweat. When he stepped safely onto the heather, I flung my arms around him, too, and felt his chest shake with relieved laughter.

Then I knelt by the crate, hiding from myself behind my hair. Talk about publicly exposing my emotions. I'd be arrested for indecency if I kept this up.

The seal pup's brown eyes peered incongruously from beneath the hem of my mohair sweater. "Pretty fancy seal," said one of the auxiliaries and the others guffawed. I heard Nicholas laughing too and I risked a quick glance through my hair. His eyes flicked toward me and kept on laughing, and that was the moment I felt a flutter of hope. Maybe now we could be friends?

CHAPTER NINE

"What will happen to the seal?" I asked, as Jeannie and Marie swung the crate into the back of the Landrover.

"Oh, we'll take him to the Seal Sanctuary at Gweek," Jeannie replied with a smile. "We'll let him have a half-hour rest, then we'll check him over and treat his wounds. I'd say he's only a week or two old, just a little guy. He was probably washed from the breeding rocks by storm waves and separated from his mom."

"You want your jumper back?" asked Marie.

My warm, expensive sweater was stretched and salty, the mohair bedraggled. One of the pup's flipper claws talk. Nicholas got two cans of orange Fanta from the fridge, and we gulped the pop down.

"Now for dessert," said Nicholas. "And don't tell me you're on some dodgy diet."

"No, I am not," I said indignantly, and he grinned at my tone.

"Don't get your knickers twisted, wench. Princesses usually eat like sparrows. Peck, peck. But I forgot — you're not a princess. Right?"

"Right."

He set a plate of raisin scones on the table, along with a pot of raspberry jam and a carton of something yellow and crusty.

"What's this stuff?" I asked.

"Clotted cream. Don't tell me you've never had it."

"I've never had it."

"If ee stay 'ere weth we, maid, you'll eat yer fair weight in cream. Tez a Cornish thing. Spread en on yer scone," he teased, reminding me of his father.

I watched as Nicholas split his scone in half, smeared each half with a generous dollop of jam, and then spooned up some cream. Under the yellow crust, it was smooth and pale. He spread spoonfuls on top of his jammy scone, opened his mouth as wide as it would go, winked at me, and slid the scone in. That shut him up. I jammed and creamed my own scone while he munched, then took a bite. Delicious — sweet jam, rich cream!

I stuffed the rest of my scone into my mouth, and Nicholas began jamming his second piece. Blondie stuck her long, cool nose into my hand and gave a nudge.

"Watch this," Nicholas said, and he held a piece of scone over Blondie's head. "Sing," he commanded, and she gave a low howl, her brown eyes melting. Nicholas gave her the scone and she ate it daintily, licking crumbs from her lips.

"I'm exhausted," I moaned. "My legs feel like rubber."

"Lucky for me and Perran you can run so fast," said Nicholas and there it was again — that admiring light in his blue eyes.

I brushed crumbs from the table and retied the bread bag in silence, since my suave rejoinder to Nicholas' compliment seemed to have got misplaced somewhere between my brain and my tongue. If my neurons were running a courier service, they'd be told to go home without pay.

"Do you want to come back to Falmouth and see where I'm staying?" I finally asked.

"Brilliant," Nicholas said. "Be ready in a jiffy — gotta get some warmer stuff on."

I talked to Blondie while he changed, stroking her smooth forehead and making her feathery tail sway to and fro. When Nicholas reappeared in black jeans and a sweatshirt, he was carrying my straw bag.

"Yes!" I exclaimed in surprise. It had never occurred to me that he might have rescued it from the boathouse.

"Here's your clobber," he said. "Lucky for you I didn't flog it."

I was learning to watch his eyes to see when he was teasing, but I still needed a dictionary. "Flog it?" I asked.

"Sell it, make myself a quid or two."

"A quid?"

"A pound — you know, money. What's the matter with you anyway? Don't they teach you to speak English in the colonies?"

"We've evolved beyond it," I said smugly, following him outside.

We walked down the lane to the bus stop slowly, because every step seemed to pull all the muscles I had in each leg. The bus arrived almost empty, and I followed Nicholas' long strides to the back seat. Here we swayed and rocked over the bumps. Sometimes our shoulders touched, but Nicholas didn't seem to notice, so I pretended that I didn't either.

I wondered if Skye would be at home. When I'd left that morning, she'd been working at the huge canvas, just as she had been when I'd gone to bed the previous evening. Had she worked on it all night? I hoped she'd be out when we arrived; I wasn't sure anymore what our relationship was. Our fight had complicated things. I didn't know what to think of her, and I didn't know what she thought of me. Maybe she disrespected me now (like I'd been disrespecting her, I thought guiltily). I didn't want all these confused emotions swirling around the first time I brought Nicholas home.

Whether Skye was there or not, it was too much to hope that the front room would be looking normal. I knew the sofa would be swathed in a paint sheet, and every surface covered in brushes and pallets daubed with blobs of hardening paint.

"So is your family with you?" Nicholas asked.

"No, just my dad's girlfriend. She's a bit — different."

"Two heads, green hair? Tattoos on her toes?"

"Get real. She's just, umm — I don't know. You'll probably meet her," I said gloomily.

"Well, don't sweat it," he said. "My father's got a woman in the house who speaks in some middle European tongue, dresses like a gypsy, and lurks around corners all the time."

"I saw her."

"Oh, yeah. That was another thing I was browned off about. Having to explain her to you. Like I know what there is to explain."

"Is she your dad's girlfriend?" I asked.

"Pretty weird setup if she is. He never pays her any attention."

"Maybe that's just when you're around."

"Perhaps." He scowled at his long fingers, clasped on his knees.

I wondered if some girl had given Nicholas the silver Celtic ring on his left hand. But it wasn't the kind of thing I could ask . . . yet. Getting to know someone is like peeling down through an onion — all those concentric rings of privacy.

"So, Dad's a bit dodgy," Nicholas said. "Usually, my mom's pretty okay. But right now she's going ballistic over Gran's estate. Like it matters which relative gets each piece of silverware and the Spode china. It's all a bunch of bollocks. I told her, if she sent me down here it would totally mess my whole summer and all my plans. But did she care? Nope. So I was browned off about that, too." He sighed and flexed his fingers.

"Anyway, enough about me. Where's your mother?" he asked.

"She's dead."

"Oh, crikey, I'm sorry! I mean, I didn't know —"

Against the window of the bus, filled with Falmouth's granite buildings, his thin face flushed under his tan. At that moment, I could have hugged him again.

"Hey, it's okay," I said lightly. "She's been gone since I was six. And here's our stop."

Listening to Nicholas' steps behind me on the apartment stairs, I wondered if asking him here had been a mistake. Was I ready to share so much of myself, the problem in my life called Skye? And had Skye forgiven my rudeness of the other night? Was I leading Nicholas right into a scene full of recriminations and roaring silences? I'd have to play it carefully, use my Survival Strategy of not getting involved, perhaps, or be super polite.

I paused outside the door, blocking Nicholas' way. "Umm, like, I'm not sure this is a good . . ." I started to splutter. Then I remembered how he'd flushed on the bus, as though he really cared about my feelings and about my mother being dead. "Welcome *chez nous*," I finished bravely instead, and turned the doorknob.

"Hello," said Skye as we walked in.

My heart sank a couple of notches. So much for making a good First Impression, I thought dismally. The front room was cluttered up with about a million tubes of paint and brushes and pieces of rag and scraps of canvas and wooden frames to stretch the canvas onto. And then there was the frame stapler lying on the floor beside three magazines about acrylic painting, and the jugs full of water to wash brushes in, sitting on the coffee table. What must Nicholas think?

Still in front of the huge canvas, Skye herself was also looking even more disheveled than usual. Her feet were bare and her hair looked as though it had been slept on for a week. The baggy man's shirt she worked in hung almost to her knees and was so covered in paint you could hardly tell the original color had been pale blue.

I gritted my teeth and decided to be super polite. "This is Nicholas Trenoweth," I said brightly.

Skye's wide smile was reassuring — if she was holding any grudges against me, she wasn't going to drag them out right now.

"Hi," said Nicholas diffidently. Then he stepped forward, craning around Skye to look at the canvas. "Did you paint this?" he asked. "Are you an artist?"

Something intense in his voice alerted me. What was going on here? Skye stepped to one side, and Nicholas stood in front of the canvas and stared at it — I mean, really stared at it. He was like a thirsty person coming out of the desert and staring at water. It was like his eyes were going to suck up the painting in one long gulp.

"Awesome," he muttered, and he wasn't saying it to me or even to Skye. He seemed to have forgotten we were there.

I was curious now. I walked up to the canvas and stared at it, too.

"It's titled *Goodbye to Atlantis*," Skye said. "And I think it's finished. I've been working on it for about thirty-six hours."

Nicholas turned to her with his eyes shining. "Stella didn't tell me," he said. "You're a real artist. I'm going to art school when I finish my A-levels. I'll probably go to the school in Falmouth and do a four-year degree. I want to be an illustrator."

"Falmouth's a good place to go," agreed Skye. "Their graduates do very well."

I stared at Nicholas in surprise. Take another layer off the onion, I thought.

"So what's this about, *Goodbye to Atlantis*?" Nicholas asked.

"There was a documentary the other night, *Lost and Golden Places* —"

"I saw it," said Nicholas. "Lyonesse, and Trevanion on his white horse escaping the water."

"Right. So this is it," Skye said.

The canvas was a mass of swirling colors and patterns, and at first I didn't understand it — Skye's style was not realistic. Shapes and colors overlapped, and things were not always in proportion. Gradually my eyes began to make sense of what they were seeing.

Most of the canvas showed a scene underneath the water, and ribbons of green and cobalt blue and aquamarine flowed across it. The water scene was filled with objects, ordinary everyday objects, and with people. The objects and the people were swirling and tumbling, some sideways, some upside down, all tangled and overlapped. At the top of the picture, in the right corner, a curling wave rushed forward with a foaming white crest. And from the white foam sprang the body of a white horse, a horse that was maybe foam turned into horse. It was leaping ahead of the wave and into a high green field strewn with flowers.

"Trevanion's horse," said Skye.

But when I looked at the rider, it wasn't a Cornishman called Trevanion. It was a woman. It was Skye herself, with her hennaed hair wind-blown and her hands tangled in the white horse's mane.

"What does it mean?" asked Nicholas.

"It's symbolic," Skye said. "In the myth, what saved Trevanion? Not just a horse. What first saved Trevanion was his ability to let go of the past. Look at the others."

Obediently, Nicholas and I stared at the underwater people, left behind in Atlantis, a country that was forever the past. Every one of them was holding onto something: a ceramic vase, the limbs of a tree, the halter of a cow, dinner plates, the leash of a dog, a bunch of flowers, a key, a pile of books, a shovel and hammer, the hand of a child — I looked at that one closely. The woman gripping the child's hand was Skye again, a dimmer, underwater image of her, the self she'd left behind when she grabbed onto the mane of the white horse. A man was tangled in the rope of a church bell. A woman clutched a house door. And then there were other people gripping each other's hands or grabbing onto someone else by a shirtsleeve or an apron. A girl was holding a golden mirror by the handle — I looked closely at that figure, too. Would it be an underwater image of me? But no, it was a girl with short black hair.

"So all these people are clinging to the past, unable to let go," Skye said. "Only Trevanion grabbed hold of something that could carry him forward into the future. He chose a white horse. I chose art. My art gave me a future. My art is Trevanion's white horse."

"Awesome," muttered Nicholas again, and he gave

Skye such a shining look that I stared at her curiously. What did he see when he looked at her golden eyes, her mop of curls, the diamond chip in her nose?

"If I brought you some of my work, would you look at it?" Nicholas asked, sounding shy.

"I'd be happy to," Skye responded cheerfully. She finished screwing caps back onto tubes of acrylic paint, then pulled the shirt off over her head. "Phew," she said, "maybe I should eat. I'm not sure when the last time was that I had anything. Have you guys eaten?"

"We had tea," I said. "English tea."

Skye smiled. "You'll be able to eat more. Let's have something else," she said. "Nicholas, can you peel some potatoes?"

"I'm fantastic with the peeler," he said. "But first, can I turn the telly on? I want to check out my dad."

"Where is he?" I asked.

"Somewhere between here and France, in the boat."

Skye and I both froze. "The boat?" I repeated, thinking of the storm.

"The forty-six-footer you saw in the cove. He's sailing in the annual race from Falmouth to La Rochelle in France. But the weather's been a bit wild."

I glanced out to the harbor, where waves were still slapping at the wall like angry hands. When Skye turned the local news channel on, we saw pictures of breached seawalls, the Coastguard rescuing three men off a fishing trawler before it sank near treacherous reefs called the Manacles, and even a brief view of orphaned seals recuperating in ponds.

I tensed up as the announcer's voice said, "The worst

August storm in memory caused havoc amongst a group
of sailors racing from Falmouth to La Rochelle. One
yachtsman was rescued by a tanker after transmitting a
Mayday signal."

The camera zoomed in on a fuzzy image of this rescue.
The announcer's voice continued: "Another contender,
from Portscatho, was winched to safety by a navy helicopter after his yacht foundered in heavy seas."

Skye and I both tried to look at Nicholas without his
noticing us. He looked pretty calm, so I guessed neither
of the boats were his father's. I couldn't remember what
the name had been on the boat I'd seen anchored in the
cove.

"Are you anxious about your father?" asked Skye.
Tactful as ever. She wandered into the kitchen as
Nicholas answered, though. Maybe she was giving him
some space.

"Nope," said Nicholas sounding nonchalant. "Dad's
been sailing ever since he was a kid. He just about lives
in the Channel and sails to France at night all the time."

"What's his boat called?" I asked.

"*Fetha*," Nicholas replied. "It's a Cornish word meaning to conquer or beat. Just right."

"What do you mean?"

"My dad, he has to win at things. Whatever it takes.
Especially if there's money involved."

"If no one's at home, you're welcome to stay here for
the night," Skye said, returning to the front room with a
potato peeler in one hand. "I'll clear the sofa for you. Is
there anyone at the house you should call?"

"Nope," said Nicholas nonchalantly again.

I thought of the woman in the garden, who complained about being in danger. Some weird friend of my dad's, Nicholas had called her. Was she sailing with Richard or had she left? Or didn't Nicholas want to call and talk to her? I bunched the questions in my mouth and swallowed them down.

CHAPTER TEN

Dear Ashley — surprise! Nicholas showed me where the computers are in Falmouth Library. For 50 pence you can use them for half an hour, so I'm using my 50 pence to e-mail you. Nicholas is taking a rented game back to the video store and then we're going to his place and he's going to teach me to windsurf. Yesterday we went to a theme park called Flambards — his dad took us in a sports car. (He was out sailing last week in an amazing storm!) He's rich, I think! He bought Nicholas and me each a cool camera, and we've been taking fab pictures of everything. I'll send some. He also took us sail-

*ing in his yacht, plus paid for us to go horse riding
on the beach at Perranporth (miles of sand and big
dunes). So eat your heart out, sister! Just kidding.
I seriously hope you are having just as much fun at
home. Did you get my cornpicking job? I hope
you're missing me because I'm missing you mucho
mucho and I've bought a fun souvenir for you but
you'll have to live in suspense until I give it to you
because it's going to be a secret until then. Nicholas
is here and the librarian is giving me the evil eye so
I'd better go now! See ya!*

Love Stella xxxxxxx

*P.S. Don't forget you can ride Malibu whenever you
want, and if you e-mail me at my usual address, I
can retrieve the mail from the library here — so
write soon with all the home gossip!*

*P.P.S. Nicholas and I went to visit a seal pup we
rescued and he's learning to eat fish now and his
coat is changing from white to brown. Nicholas
sketched pictures of him. Librarian about to
explode — death imminent. Send pink roses for my
funeral!*

S xxxx

I slung my bag over my shoulder and followed Nicholas
out into the sunshine. Falmouth Library faces into something called The Moor. It's like a town square, where
markets used to be held. These days, it's a humungous
parking lot, plus a space where taxis and buses line up,
and where pigeons and seagulls stroll around looking for

handouts. The birds scurried out of our way as we dashed for the Maen Porth bus and flung ourselves, panting, into the last row of seats.

Nicholas pulled a sticky-looking bag from one pocket and thrust it toward me.

"Want one?"

I peered into the bag cautiously, then took a big cookie, gooey with cherries, toffee, and nuts all held together by a thick chocolate coating on the bottom.

"Yum."

"Florentines," said Nicholas around a chewy mouthful. Then, "Who does this remind you of?" he asked.

I took the furled newspaper he handed me, and examined the photo on the front page. A woman wearing a flower print dress and a head scarf was shown standing on a city street with a small child. The woman's face, with high cheek bones, had a gaunt look and there was a proud but anxious expression in her eyes.

"Do I know her?" I asked. "She looks kind of familiar."

"Read the caption," Nicholas said, licking his fingers.

A Romanian refugee begging in London, the small print under the photo read.

Opposition claims Britain's social systems burdened to breaking point by illegal immigrants. Full story, page 2.

"Read it," said Nicholas.

I grappled the paper open to page 2, folding its rustling sheets into some kind of crumpled submission. *ILLEGAL IMMIGRANTS REACH FLOOD PRO-PORTIONS. ACTION NEEDED NOW!* shouted the headline. I scanned the columns below, while the bus jolted under me and the pages shook in my hands.

Critics contend the government is ignoring the most serious issue facing Britain today: the flood of illegal immigrants arriving by lorry and boat from Sri Lanka, Africa, Eastern Europe, and China. While a high percentage of illegals enter by deceiving an immigration officer, others are smuggled in. Eighty-four percent arrive via Dover, where a recent tragedy involved thirty-two Sri Lankans dead in the back of a refrigerator truck. Human trafficking is "big business," says a source at The National Criminal Intelligence Service (NCIS), and takes place on the scale of organized crime, with links to the Mafia. However, even "amateur smugglers," with no links to international rings, may smuggle human cargo into the country on a sporadic basis to obtain quick profits. This smuggling may involve personal vehicles or boats. A recent initiative sees criminal and intelligence officers joining forces to form a special, multitask squad charged with tackling the issue of human trafficking.

Nicholas reached past the paper and pulled the bell cord, letting the bus driver know that we wanted to climb out at the next stop. I folded the paper up and shoved it into my bag, feeling mystified.

"Why did you want me to read it?" I asked Nicholas as we set off down the lane.

"Who did the Romanian woman in the photo remind you of?" he asked.

"I'm not sure."

"What about my dad's friend, who lurks around the house?"

"What —?"

I stopped to pull out the paper and take another look, making a mental comparison. "It's not her," I said. "This is a younger woman."

"I know that," said Nicholas. "But the two women look alike. Same expression. Same clothes. And Romanian is an eastern European language. Have you heard my dad's friend talk?"

"Only a few words. But she does have a strong accent."

"Exactly," said Nicholas grimly.

"What are you getting at?" I asked.

"What if she's a refugee and Dad's hiding her? But why would he do that? Why would he be mixed up with refugees?"

For a few minutes we walked in puzzled silence. The high hedges sheltered us from the breeze and the air was very warm, carrying the scent of cow parsley flowers and ploughed earth and a salty tang. High overhead a skylark warbled its twittering song and a cow mooed in a field. Bees buzzed in the furze bushes. The world of international crime seemed like a plot element in a thriller movie set someplace else, faraway.

"Maybe she is your dad's girlfriend."

"When I caught the bus home from your place last Tuesday," Nicholas said, "I saw something."

"What?"

"I saw my dad coming out of The Grape's Inn with his arm around a blonde woman. They were laughing, then they got in his car and had a quick snog and drove away —"

"Snog?" I asked.

Nicholas rolled his eyes. "Kiss, you colonial," he said.

"Oh. Whatever."

"So I don't think this woman staying at the house is Dad's girlfriend. I think the blonde is his girlfriend."

"Maybe your dad's helping the woman out," I suggested. "You know, because he's a nice guy and he's being kind to her. Or she could be just a friend," I argued. "Or maybe she's working for your dad. Does she do any cooking and cleaning? Maybe she's a housekeeper."

"If she's a friend," said Nicholas, "where did Dad meet her? And why is she hanging around the house? If she's a housekeeper, she'd have to do some work. But she doesn't . . . she doesn't do any work."

"She gardens," I protested, remembering the day I'd seen her weeding the terraces. But that reminded me of something else. I told Nicholas about the conversation I'd overheard between the foreign woman and Richard, when the woman complained about being in danger.

"What?!" said Nicholas. He stopped in his tracks and fixed me with an intense stare. It was sort of like being a deer in a car's headlights. "Are you sure that's what the woman said?" he asked.

"Of course, I'm sure. She said 'Is danger here' and your dad told her things were fine and he'd talk to his contact Jean Paul. Do you know Jean Paul?"

"No. He sounds French. Dad has lots of friends in Brittany and Normandy. He's always sailing over there. When my mother and I lived here, we used to go camping in France in the summer hols."

"Well, I'm sure there's a logical explanation to it all," I said stiffly. "I mean, your dad's not going to be doing anything wrong, is he?"

Nicholas gave his hair a shake and didn't reply.

"Come on, chill out and forget about it," I said, but Nicholas strode beside me in dogged silence.

I thought about Richard with his sports car and his music and his golden dog; about the cameras he'd bought us and the horse rides he'd paid for; about how he teased me while he let me stand at the wheel of his yacht in the wind and sunshine of Falmouth Bay. He'd taken us out for supper too, and bought me a boyband CD. His lean, tanned face always lit up when I arrived at Rose Mullion, and he'd made me feel at home there: lighting coal fires on cool evenings and showing me how to rig the sailing dinghies. He made me feel like a girl in a movie or a photo shoot — he looked classy in his expensive clothes, a silk scarf knotted at his throat, his continental jackets flung over one shoulder. He was like the men who lounged in the background of magazine pictures, slightly out of focus behind the models but ready to step into the foreground whenever the models turned and called their names.

It was too far out to imagine that words like "illegal immigration" and "human trafficking" lay beneath the surface of Richard's perfect life.

"Will your wet suit fit me? I'm going to —" I began to say, but suddenly Nicholas turned and grabbed my arm and yanked me sideways. Startled and off balance, I fell onto him in the grass and he laid his fingers across my mouth.

"Listen," he whispered fiercely.

I shook hair from my eyes. We had almost reached the gravel parking spot behind Rose Mullion when Nicholas grabbed me. To one side of this area, a sagging stone wall enclosed what had once been a garden. Now long grass filled it, but in places, tenacious onions struggled to lift their purple flowers into the light. The garden gate was missing, and the wall leaned against a rough granite post covered with orange lichen. Nicholas and I were behind the wall, flattening the long grass. He inched his face toward the granite gatepost and stared around it.

I pulled my arm away from him and rubbed it.

There were voices in the parking area.

"Won't be long now. Tez all set for this weekend." That was Peter, the van driver who'd taken me home, the man with a smile like a lighthouse beam and words like cold sea currents.

"All come?" asked a woman's anxious voice. I recognized the guttural accent and tensed, suddenly understanding Nicholas' dive behind the wall. The foreign woman was in the yard, talking to Peter.

A vehicle door closed. The voices were muffled. Then I heard, "Right-o, darling. We'll soon 'ave ee all together again and upcountry."

"Country? England?" faltered the woman.

"Es, get yer into England with yer old man and yer dad," said Peter. "Tez all fixed for the weekend. Four days," he said — trying to make the woman understand how long it was until the weekend.

There was the sound of gravel crunching underfoot, then silence. The sea sighed against the rocks below the cliffs, and Nicholas' rigid back relaxed. He sank onto his heels, beside me in the grass.

"What did all that mean?" he asked. "What's fixed for the weekend?"

"I don't know. You've got lichen on your face."

He brushed it away absentmindedly but there were still marks on his skin where the rock had imprinted its sharp crystals.

I leaned my back against the wall, hoping Nicholas would notice how close we'd been together in the grass, how secret the old garden was, how summery and Seriously Mature I looked lounging in the sunshine. But he only stared at a leaf in his hand, tearing it into little strips. Whatever he was thinking about, it wasn't me.

"I'm getting a cramp in my leg," I complained. Besides, this was dumb. Like a kid game of spies and bad guys, like something Noah used to get me to play in the barn and the paddock while Pearl cooked our supper and Dad wrote learned papers in his study. I stood up and brushed grass pollen off my leggings.

When we emerged from behind the wall, I saw the white antiques truck standing by the house. Peter and the woman were nowhere in sight. The back door to the truck was open and Nicholas wandered over to it and looked in. Suddenly he motioned for me to follow, and he jumped up inside. I leaned against the tailgate and looked in. Rolls of carpet and heavy flannel cloth, for wrapping around antiques and preventing scratches, were piled against one wall. A small manila tag, with the words "Lot 29" printed on it in black, lay near me on the floor.

"Look at this!" Nicholas exclaimed. "It's a secret compartment!"

Across the front of the truck's interior, a partition had

been built from floor to ceiling. Nicholas swung the door in the partition wide and climbed inside; in the cupboardlike space, there was room for several people if they didn't mind being squished together. When Nicholas climbed back out and swung the partition door shut, I could hardly tell the secret space existed. The door fit so snugly and perfectly.

Steps crunched in the gravel and my heart leaped.

"Someone's coming," I hissed, and Nicholas sprang across the truck floor and landed on the gravel beside me. We were just turning away from the truck when Peter strode around the corner of the house. His eyes narrowed in a scowl when he saw us, and I imagined his mermaid tattoo coiling and lashing her tail.

"Hi!" I said, using my super-polite, impress-the-teacher voice, but Peter ignored me.

"If yer looking for yer dad, 'e's up to Bodmin to a sale," he said to Nicholas.

"I know," Nicholas replied.

"Then watcher 'anging around gawping at?" Peter asked belligerently. "Tez time they fools in London changed the school year to include the summertime. Too much 'anging around and not enough work gets done by the likes of you all summer."

Nicholas flushed and his thin lips tightened, but he didn't say anything, just stared at Peter. The man hawked up and spat into the gravel, then swung into the driver's seat and slammed the door.

"Yer dog's barking 'er 'ead off," he said, and then the engine roared into life with such a burst of energy that I flinched. Peter must've had his foot on the gas pedal like a bag of cement. The truck lurched up the lane and Nicholas continued to stare after it.

"What was all that about?" I asked.

"Dunno. Peter was in a right state about something. I don't think he liked us being around the lorry. Maybe he was afraid we'd seen the secret compartment. What would it be used for?"

I followed Nicholas to the door, where he let Blondie outside to join us, then we continued on around the house and down through the garden. The broken twigs and palm fronds had been cleared away after the storm, and the garden was peaceful and scented with flowers.

"What would Peter hide in the compartment?" Nicholas asked again. "You know, once the lorry was loaded full of furniture, no one could tell the compartment was there. You could stack stuff right up against it and cover it all with carpets."

"Peter's a bit strange, isn't he?" I asked.

"Strange?"

"Always going on about Cornwall for the Cornish and emmetts and things."

Nicholas laughed. "Lots of Cornish from old families think like that," he said. "It's partly why the Cornish have always smuggled stuff — it's a way of telling the English lawmakers to get stuffed. Anyway me 'andsome, you'm part Cornish yerself."

"Yes, I guess." I hadn't thought about this much; as we scrambled down the path to the cove, I tried to figure out how much Cornish blood flowed in my veins.

"Do the Cornish still smuggle?" I asked.

"Es, me dear maid. When the fishing trawlers do come into Newlyn, they be loaded to the 'atches with cocaine and heroin and other stuff as do blow yer mind."

I giggled. "What about Romanian women?" I asked.

"Oh es, wummen. We do like wummen in these parts," Nicholas said, licking his lips. "But ef you squeal to the English, you'll wish you'd kept yer trap shut." He drew his fingers across his throat in a slicing gesture and leaped down onto the beach with a laugh.

I lingered behind, looking at the sea. It was slack tide and only a gentle swell licked lightly at the rocks. Stars of light glittered on the swell and on the golden weed stirring in the deep green water off the headland. Richard's white yacht dipped lazily at her anchor. Out near the horizon a tanker steamed slowly northward up the channel.

Since the storm, I hadn't trusted the sea. It was hard to forget how the water had pounded the rocks and surged into the other cove, trapping Nicholas. It was hard now to look at the water and not wonder what lay below its smooth surface; what battered ships and drowned sailors, what towers and roofs of a lost Atlantis were concealed by spangled sunlight.

I gave myself a shake. A tortoiseshell butterfly floated past me, and the montbretia flowers at the edge of the path opened their orange trumpets. This afternoon the sea was as lazy and supple as a cat in the drowsy warmth. I might even manage the Windsurfer. I jumped down onto the grating shingle and headed after Nicholas, stripping my shirt off from over my yellow bikini.

CHAPTER ELEVEN

The next day, we caught the little train to St. Ives, where my great-grandmother had been born. The train was only two coaches in length, and pulled out of St. Erth station with a lurch. I blinked as the bright morning sun slid across my face, then put my shades on. The train picked up speed, swaying rhythmically, its wheels clattering over points. Soon we were beside the sea, running along the cliffs on a single track.

"Wow!" I pressed my face to the window, staring at miles of golden sand surrounding a huge bay filled with brilliant blue-green sea and a distant lighthouse standing proudly erect on a dark, jagged rock.

"This is awesome!" I said, but Nicholas didn't reply. He was wearing shades, too, and his face was still and cool against the blue plush of the train seats. I stretched out my leg and nudged his foot.

"Earth to Nicholas," I said, but he didn't smile. "What's the matter?" I asked. "You're like a million miles away. You're not freezing over, are you?"

He shrugged, the way horses shrug to dislodge flies.

"What?" I persisted.

"When we get to St. Ives, we're going to have to walk a long way," he said. "Princess, I don't see how you're going to walk in three-inch platforms. And if we go surfing, your jewelry will get lost or nicked off the beach."

"No, it won't," I said stubbornly.

I twisted my six silver bangles, threaded with blue beads, around on my wrist. Matching earrings clinked softly when I moved my head. I was having a Seriously Mature day, but I didn't feel like explaining myself. For days, Nicholas and I had been hanging out and I'd been in my grade-two mood, not caring about the scratches on my nails, not even getting upset when I tore a hole in my white Capri pants as we explored a cave in the cliffs. But this morning, I'd woken up thinking about my great-grandmother and then about my mother. I'd stared at her framed picture by my bed, and then I'd known I had to smarten up. I had to get serious.

"Stella, you're very pretty," Nicholas said. "But you don't have to work so hard to impress me. What I really need right now is a friend."

"I *am* your friend," I said defensively. "And I don't see how my clothes are any of your business." I stuck my jaw out at him, but he was following some thoughts of his own.

"You know, I was really close to my gran," Nicholas said. "And it's a bit weird staying at my dad's. He totally doesn't want me around."

"How can you say that? He's been super kind."

"Kind to you. He likes having you around because then I'm occupied and he can ignore me. All he wants to do is work or sail that dumb boat. He's going off on it this coming weekend. And before he left for work this morning, he gave me a going-over about 'not bothering Peter and getting in his way when he has work to do and staying out of the lorry.'"

I pondered Nicholas' words, while the train rocked past a fishing trawler in the sea below. A cloud of raucous gulls swirled around it.

"Peter must have told him," I said.

"Yeah. And then, last night, Dad was going on in French on the phone. He didn't know I was in the house."

"What did he say?"

"I didn't get all of it because my French is a bit dodgy. But there was something about 'two people coming,' and 'twenty-one hundred hours.'"

"Maybe he was talking to Jean Paul, his friend."

"His contact," corrected Nicholas.

"What do you think it all meant?"

"I think it's something to do with refugees or illegal immigrants. Maybe he gives them rides in the lorry."

"Are you serious? Come off it." How could Nicholas sit there, looking so calm and matter-of-fact, and say such bizarre things about his own father?

"Why would he be helping people like that?" I asked.

"I dunno. But think about it. He has a van with a secret compartment, and a woman waiting for something to happen, and Peter told the woman that her old man and her father would be going upcountry with her this weekend."

"That doesn't prove anything," I protested. "The compartment might have been in the truck when your dad bought it. Or maybe he stows his personal stuff there when he's traveling. Or maybe Peter and the woman are friends and Peter is giving her and her family a ride. So what?"

"So, maybe you're right. Or not," Nicholas said.

"Why don't you just ask your dad about it?"

"When I asked him about the woman, he kind of scowled at me and muttered something about her being a friend and then he changed the subject."

"Maybe he doesn't even know about the compartment in the truck," I suggested. "Maybe that's something to do with Peter. Or maybe it's a place where they transport small antiques, breakable things."

"Possibly," Nicholas said, but he didn't sound convinced. He twisted his silver ring around on his finger with a puzzled frown.

Boys! I thought in exasperation. Everything had to be good guys and bad guys, like life was a movie or a video game. I didn't want to even suspect that there was anything hidden in Richard's perfect life; I wanted to hold onto the image of him laughing in his sports car. He was one of the good guys, wasn't he?

"Get real," I said to Nicholas. "You're just trying to make up a mystery. I'm sure everything's fine."

Nicholas scowled at me, and I turned away and stared out the window. I hadn't forgiven him yet for commenting on my clothes; if I didn't start ignoring him, he might wreck my mood. In the periphery of my vision, he pulled his sketchpad from his pack and began to draw something — I didn't ask what.

Ahead, beyond the curve of a small headland, I saw the fishing town of St. Ives poking its long finger into the bay. White buildings and pale sand shone in the sun. This place had been my great-grandmother's home. It was beautiful.

The rhythm of the train wheels changed as we slowed and pulled into St. Ives station. Passengers piled out, blinking in the sun. I sniffed the salty wind. Palm trees lined a long beach with green-and-white changing huts, and on a rocky headland, a white hotel faced the bay.

Nicholas hitched his pack onto his shoulder, and we began walking silently into the town. I stretched my legs out long, determined to prove I could walk just as fast as him, despite my three-inch platforms. We threaded narrow streets where window boxes full of bright flowers advertised bed-and-breakfasts in old fishermen's cottages.

A crowd of tourists jostled toward us: children sucking on long sticks of striped candy, mothers in straw hats, fathers in bright shirts. I stepped aside to let them pass. An old, tiled drain bordered the narrow street, and I teetered on the edge of it. A sharp pain stabbed through one ankle as my heel slipped from my platform sandal.

I stayed still after the tourists had passed, waiting for the pain to subside. I didn't think it was serious, hopefully not a sprain. Gingerly, I tested the ankle with my weight and then set off carefully after Nicholas.

"Don't walk so fast," I complained, and Nicholas swung back to face me.

"I'm not walking fast."

I sat down on the steps leading into a tiny garden and pulled my shoes off and shoved them into my bag. Nicholas didn't say anything. If he'd said, "I told you so," I would have walked back to the train and gone home. Instead, he sat beside me on the step.

"Why don't you buy some thongs? I know a place that sells them."

I nodded, feeling miserable. It was hot, and the town was filled with people in shorts and bathing suits. I knew I didn't fit in; that I should have dressed more casually, that Nicholas was right about my shoes. I wiped the back of my hand across my mouth, smearing off plum-colored lipstick. When I'd dressed that morning and painted my fingernails and toenails "Luscious Plum with Sparkles," I'd felt sophisticated, a woman of the world. Now I just felt like a little kid playing dress-up with clothes borrowed from an adult's closet. A little kid who should have stayed at home. Majorly dorky.

I stared at my purple toenails. I wished I was back home in the barn, grooming Malibu, my hands smelling like horse and my soft old jeans grubby against my thighs. Things seemed simple in the barn, with only a horse for company, with the swallows nesting in the rafters that my grandfather had hammered into place. In the barn, I knew exactly who I was and how to act. Outside the barn, I thought, life was a mystery — but not a game.

"It's because of my mother," I said suddenly.

"What is?"

"She was a fashion designer," I explained. "She always looked totally gorgeous. And now she's dead, but I'm her only daughter. I feel like . . . I kind of owe it to her or something. To follow in her footsteps. Like, now that I'm older, I'm always trying to please her and think about what she would approve of. I guess that sounds pretty dumb," I finished lamely.

"No."

"Well, it probably is dumb. Anyway, just so you know."

I stood up, hefting my shoes in the straw bag, and began to pad barefoot down the hot cobbled alleyway leading toward the harbor. Nicholas caught up to me and reached for my hand. Surprise tingled through me. His grip was strong and warm, and comfort seemed to flow out of it and up my arm like an electrical current.

"Hey, Stella, I'm sorry. About the princess thing," he said. "Friends?"

"Friends," I agreed. "And I'm sorry for what I said about your dad — you know, about making up a mystery. Maybe you're right and there's something weird going on."

"I don't really know him anymore," Nicholas said. "He doesn't want to talk to me or have me around. He's only happy with me when I'm away somewhere. It's like I make him nervous."

I gave Nicholas' hand a sympathetic squeeze but I didn't know what to say. I couldn't imagine my father not wanting me around. I couldn't imagine Richard, dressed like a hero, being a bad guy.

We were down by the harbor now, where bright fishing boats tilted at crazy angles on the rippled sand exposed by low tide. The beach was crowded with tourists lying on towels behind striped canvas windbreakers. Seagulls strutted and mewed, watching children with ice cream cones. I bought thongs at a shop selling plastic buckets and spades in bright colors.

"So, you want to check out the arcade next?" Nicholas asked.

"Sure."

The arcade was dim when we ducked into it. Lights flashed in time to the music's bass beat. We played a car-racing game and Nicholas beat me three times. Then we played two shooting games and I won them both. All my shots were bull's eyes.

"Alright!" Nicholas said in admiring surprise.

"Noah, my twin, taught me," I explained.

"Do you miss him?" Nicholas asked curiously.

"Yeah, sometimes. It's a bit weird being so far apart. It's this feeling all the time that something is missing."

When we ran out of change we wandered along by the harbor, past art galleries and shops selling souvenirs. Outside an ancient pub called The Sloop, people sat on the ground or leaned against walls, drinking steins of dark beer. A collie dog wearing a red bandana slept in the shade.

"People here can take their drinks outside?" I asked in surprise.

"Why not?" Nicholas said. "Let's get lunch."

He pointed to a sign, The Balancing Eel, and we lined up in the fish-and-chip shop underneath it. The air was thick with grease and the sizzling of food in oil. A woman with plump arms doused our food with vinegar, waved a saltshaker over it, and wrapped everything in newspaper. We carried the packages outside and sat on a bench by the water.

"These fries are different," I said.

"They're chips not fries, you colonial. What's different about them?"

"They're soggier and bigger than fries at home. But good," I hastened to add. When the fish and chips were all eaten, we threw the newspaper into a trashcan and bought ice cream cones with long pieces of flaky chocolate stuck into them. For some reason, they were called Ninety-nines. In a souvenir shop, I found a model fishing boat for Noah and a box of Cornish Cream Toffees for Pearl.

Nicholas led the way to a rental shop on Fore Street, and I slipped my six bracelets and my earrings off and hid them in the bottom of my bag. Then I struggled into the black rubber tightness of a wet suit and surveyed myself critically in the mirror on the changing room door. I looked like a character from a video game — one of those tough females toting a handgun and leaping from catwalks and snarling things to their inferiors in a Russian accent. I was a bit too flat in the chest for the role but my legs, in the changing room mirror, looked good — legs that could grip a bareback horse and run over rocks to save a seal. I hoped my legs kind of balanced out my chest on some invisible scorecard.

I ran my hand across my stomach. It was okay: pretty flat. I wondered if I'd have the willpower to diet if I needed to. At school, there were girls who ate only celery at lunch, and others who ate nothing at all but sipped Diet Cokes slowly to make them last through the twenty-minute break. How did they do it, while all around them the boys wolfed pizza slices and cheese sticks and sticky pieces of cake and yummy candy bars? And I, from the corner of my eye, watched the girls and pretended not to. Even to myself, it was hard to admit that I might be fascinated by them, even jealous of them. Such control, such power over their bodies! At the same time, I felt superior because I had a flat tummy without any effort, but a little voice in my mind said, You'd do it, too, if you had to. You're no better than them, just luckier.

"Yo! You dead in there?" Nicholas asked outside the door, jolting me into the present.

"Chill," I said, "I'm coming."

Nicholas rented two boogie boards painted with fluorescent green patterns, and we headed across the narrow neck of St. Ives to Porth Meor beach on the north shore. This faced the open sea, and white rollers curled in speckled with the black bodies of surfers. This was the sea in yet another mood, I realized, and decided to trust myself to it.

We plunged into the waves.

"Yow!" I yelled. "It's freezing!"

But I didn't stop. Waves swirled against my legs, tugging and pushing. Sun glittered in my eyes and suddenly I began to laugh, throwing myself forward into the playful sea. It reminded me of an animal again, something huge and joyful frolicking in the heat. It splashed past my chest and a breaker rushed at me, frothing like a milkshake. I flung myself stomach down on the boogie board, the way I'd seen Nicholas do it, and the wave surged under the board. My feet left the bottom and I careened wildly toward the shore, riding slick as a seal on the water.

Nicholas, plunging back into deeper water, slapped my hand in a high five as he passed. I thrust out after him while water crashed around me. Cool! This was the best thing I'd done in Cornwall yet! My lips tasted of salt and sun, and my whole body felt playful and alive. I stood on tiptoe in water up to my chin and waited for the next lazy swell to surge under me, lifting me on its back, shooting me to the hot sand.

Finally, we both staggered up the beach, tired in every muscle. Sand coated my wet feet and the dull roar of surf surged to and fro in my head. I rummaged in the bottom of my bag and checked that my jewelry was still safely there, but I didn't put it back on. In the wet suit, I felt as though I blended in on the beach — one more person fooling around, not having to figure things out. In the surf, things were simple, the way they were in the barn at home. The beach, I thought, was one of those places where at any age, you were allowed simply to play. Maybe that was why I loved it.

"I'm famished!" I said cheerfully.

"Yeah, me too. Shall we buy more chips?"

"Yup! But first let's find my great-grandmother's house."

CHAPTER TWELVE

We hitched the boogie boards under our tired arms and headed back into the narrow streets, hemmed in by rows of fishermen's cottages with brightly painted doors and window frames.

My thongs flapped against my heels with every step, and I knew that the sea had washed away all my makeup. My hair, which I'd shampooed and blow-dried so carefully in the morning, was sticky with salt and plastered against my neck in wet tendrils. I felt free and tingly with happiness. I remembered that part of me belonged here, in this old town by the sea, where my great-grandmother had been born and had listened to the roar of the surf.

"It says in Maggie's journal that her house was in a street called The Digey," I said. "The house is called Gull's Roost now."

"I know The Digey. Turn here," Nicholas said. I followed him up the cobbled street, through its blue shadows.

"This is the downlong part of St. Ives," he told me. "It's where all the fishermen used to live. And here's Gull's Roost."

It was a narrow cottage with only one window on each of the two floors. A brass knocker shaped like a dolphin gleamed on the blue door, and the granite walls were washed pale yellow. "Bed and Breakfast, No Vacancy" read a hand-printed notice in the lower window.

I narrowed my eyes and tried to imagine how things would have looked in 1904, the year my great-grandmother Maggie lived here. Skye had bought me a book of old photographs that she'd found in a secondhand bookstore, and so I knew a little about the history of St. Ives. In 1904, I thought, this cottage would've been grubbier, without bright paint and lace curtains. The narrow street would have been filled with fishermen and donkeys instead of tourists. The cobbles would have been slimy with fish scales. The harbor sand would've been crowded with luggers, the traditional Cornish fishing boats. On the harbor wall, men would have been repairing fishing nets.

I tried to imagine my great-grandmother as a scrappy girl, running in the streets with her golden red hair blowing in the wind. It all felt so distant. How had she managed, sent away across the ocean to Canada, a land where she knew nothing, where she was like a boat cast adrift? How had she managed to take charge of her life, her own future? I wished suddenly that she had lived longer, long enough for me to ask her. But like my mother, she had left me too soon. My grandmother, the woman in between, had moved to Vancouver Island before I was born. She was divorced and traveled compulsively: cruises to Alaska and the Caribbean, long weekends in Paris and Florence with a bewildering succession of male friends. Pearl referred sourly to her as a "glamour puss" but I didn't really know her. And so, I was on my own with my questions.

When I finally turned to Nicholas, I saw that he was sketching the dolphin knocker. His pencil strokes were loose and confident. "Nice," I said admiringly. It was like magic, the way he made pictures appear at the tips of his long fingers.

"Thanks," he replied, flipping the sketchpad shut and slipping it into his pack. "Now let's take the rentals back and then have chips."

Twenty minutes later, we carried hot packages from The Balancing Eel into the sandy harbor. The tide was coming in, swilling around the end of the harbor wall, under the white lighthouse. Nicholas and I found a hot rock to lean against, close to three arches in the harbor wall. I ate my chips, then wiped my greasy fingers on my towel and searched through my bag for the familiar shape of Maggie's journal.

"Look," I said. I held the book open to the first page, the photo of Harold and Maggie standing in St. Ives harbor, with the lighthouse behind them.

"It must have been strange coming back after so long away in Canada," Nicholas mused.

"Listen to what she wrote," I said. "*The past is another country, one I never expected to return to. Cornwall is my past, a vague memory of white sand and thrashing sea, the place where my childhood security was shattered by the death of my parents, the place from which I had to go forth and shape a new life, learning to let things go before I could claim my future.*"

"Like Trevanion," said Nicholas, crumpling up his chip papers and popping open a can of Tango.

"What?"

"You know, that bloke Trevanion who escaped from Atlantis on a white horse. Skye said he got away because he let the past go. What did your great-grandmother have to let go of?"

"The death of her parents, I guess. The loss of her home."

I hugged my knees and thought this over while Nicholas chugged his pop, his Adam's apple sliding up and down his throat.

"Also, Maggie was separated from her twin sister, Thomasina," I continued. "I read all about it in her journal. She was sent away to work on a farm in Canada, and her sister stayed here with relatives. Maggie liked Canada but she couldn't make a new life there until she'd found her twin and let go of her hurt and anger at their separation. See, she thought the relatives must've loved Thomasina more than they loved her. So she had to make her peace with her twin."

Nicholas smoothed his towel out and lay down on his

stomach, his back lean and brown. I spread my towel beside him and lay down, too. The sun was hot on my closed eyelids but a feathery breeze tickled my vertebrae. Seagulls called overhead, and there was a gentle wash of sound from the sea.

"If Maggie hadn't let the past go," I said, "she might not have stayed in Canada. Then I wouldn't have been born there. I would have been born in Cornwall instead. Only I wouldn't have been me. I would've been someone else."

My mind tried to work its way around this thought, an idea with a shape that it couldn't recognize. Who would I have been if my great-grandmother hadn't got her life sorted out? She might never have married Harold, her school sweetheart, or owned a flower shop, or had four children. One of these four was my grandmother, Beth, who now lived in a condo, but had once married a farmer with a pink granite house surrounded by hay and cornfields . . . the house where Noah and Dad and I live. Next in line came my mother, Katherine. After high school she had left the pink granite farmhouse for college in the city of Toronto, and made a name for herself in the fashion world working with international designers, flying to and from New York.

But Maggie, kind and tough and determined to the end of her days, had got herself sorted out in time to become my great-grandmother. And so here I was, lying on the hot sand of her first home, Stella MacLeod with dyed auburn hair and long, skinny legs.

I squinted at the little blonde hairs glinting on the brown skin of my arm. This is the arm of Stella MacLeod from Ontario, Canada, said a voice in my head. There seemed something miraculous about the pronouncement; just being alive in my own body was a mystery.

I turned my thoughts back to Maggie. Had she and Harold sat here on the sand when they came back in 1962? Had it felt miraculous to revisit the past?

"Nicholas?"

He grunted.

"Maggie came back to St. Ives," I said. "But Trevanion couldn't ever go back to Atlantis. It was gone forever."

"The St. Ives that Maggie remembered from 1904 was gone forever, too. It wouldn't have been the same in 1962 when she came back. Tourist grunge instead of fishing. And she couldn't make her parents alive again, so her past was gone forever, just like Atlantis."

I opened my eyes and looked at Nicholas lying beside me. His face was close to mine. His blue eyes were still, deep pools of color. I wanted to jump into them, to trust myself to them like a body diving into deep water.

"About my mother," I said. "She's part of my past, right?"

"Yes."

"And I don't really want to, you know, let her go. I've got this album full of photos of her, and I keep studying them, trying to figure out what she would want me to do, what kind of a person I should be to please her. So I've always planned to be a model or maybe a singer or an actress . . . but just lately, I'm not so sure. I mean, is that what she would've wanted for me? How do I know, Nicholas?"

His blue eyes held me in a long, close silence.

"My mom teaches computers at college," he said at

last. "She's pretty glam, a city woman I guess, although she grew up in Cornwall. She says it was too quiet down here, nothing happening. She's a career woman. She always gets tarted up for work: spike heels, executive suits. But you know what she tells me?"

"What?"

"She always tells me 'Follow your own instincts.'"

"So maybe that's like what Trevanion did? His heart told him to grab hold of the white horse and hold on tight?"

"Yeah. Skye said her white horse was her art and I think it's going to be the same for me. I really know I can do it, Stella. I'm going to be an illustrator someday, with books with my name on the cover. I'm not bragging about this. I just feel inside myself that I can do it, it's what I was meant to do."

"I don't know what I'm meant to do, though. It's all tangled up with my mother."

"But you have to listen to yourself, Stella. Figure out what you want. I'm not dissing your memories of your mother — but it's your life, not your mother's, that you've got to live. You've got to find your own white horse, your own way into the future."

"Yeah, I guess."

I closed my eyes again and my mother was there, under my lids. All those photos that I carried around in an album in my heart, opening their pages under my lids. Was it for myself or for her that I went to Toronto the previous summer and spent three weeks at modeling school? That I was learning to flex my voice up and down stairways of notes? That I painted my nails "Luscious

Plum with Sparkles"? That I played the flute she'd owned as a girl? Tears slid out, tickling my lashes.

"I don't want to let her go," I whispered. "Whenever I try to think about my future, I go back into the past. And I like it there, Nicholas. 'Cause my mother is always smiling. She thinks I'm a star."

For the second time that day, Nicholas reached for my hand and wove my fingers into his grip. "Hey, it's alright," he whispered.

"I've got to get my act together," I said. "I've got to get it figured out. It's so complicated."

Nicholas squeezed my fingers. I held on tightly.

I'm not a star, I thought in the black space inside my head. I know there's no star quality about my voice; it's just a clear teen voice that's a little better than my friends' voices because I've had training. And there's nothing starlike about how I play the flute. And at modeling school, a tiny part of me felt dumb all the time. Dumb and lost.

But how could I admit these things to my mother, waiting in that album inside my heart? I couldn't tell her. She'd be so disappointed in me. I was a fake, a failure.

"Hey, Stella," said Nicholas softly. "You okay?"

"I guess."

I opened my eyes and the tears on my lashes reflected the light into a thousand diamonds that quivered over Nicholas' face. I let go of Nicholas' hand and pressed a corner of towel to my eyes, then rolled over and sat up.

The boats in the harbor were afloat now, lifted by the tide. Families were packing up their picnics and beach toys, children's sandy wet clothes and striped windbreakers. Soon they would be straggling into guest houses and hotels, sunburned and tired. The sky was hazy and golden in the west, over the rooftops of St. Ives that climbed the hill above the sea.

"I'm going to look for shells," I said, scrambling to my feet. I needed a break from all these heavy thoughts that pressed me small and flat. Wandering along the highest tide mark, I scanned the sand. Pieces of colored glass were worn opaque and smooth by the sea. Red crab claws made bright exclamations amongst the scribbles of dry seaweed. Every so often my fingers would close around a small shell, brown or golden with thin white stripes.

When I reached the arches in the harbor wall, I found that the sea had piled the shingle and shells into heaps. I crunched slowly across them. It was cool in the blue shadows under the arches, and the sound of waves echoed off the stones. I climbed the shingle to the far end, where wooden timbers had been built up to hold back neap tides. Leaning on the timbers, I could look across the bay to misty blue headlands and the white lighthouse on its jagged rock. Peace descended over me slowly, like a blanket woven of light.

Nicholas crunched up to stand beside me. We watched the green ocean swells curl into white waves and slide across the bay toward us, finally washing against the other side of the timbers with a soft whoosh. Sometimes, at home in Ontario, the wind would whip the lakes into roughness, scattered with small whitecaps. But I had never experienced the beauty of Atlantic rollers until this summer. The wide, curling rollers that came creaming in so smoothly, row upon row. I felt as though I could watch them forever.

"When I was a kid," I said, "my mother used to read me a story about white horses running on the tops of the waves."

"There's a story set in St. Ives, where a sand horse sculptured on the beach turns into a wave horse and gallops away on the water," Nicholas said. "Here, I found you a shell."

It was a pink scallop shell, flat and ridged like a fan. I slipped it into my pocket, like slipping the memory of this moment into my mind — the soft echo of the sea, Nicholas' eyes, the salty taste of the air. The peacefulness I needed.

"Stella, you know what I think?"

"What?"

"See way out there in the sea, where the sky meets the water?"

I squinted through the salty haze and nodded.

"Out there, a wave is getting ready to turn into a horse. It's for you. It will come galloping across the bay to you, and when it gets here, you'll recognize it and grab hold of its mane."

"That's very deep," I said. "Maybe you should be a poet."

But I wanted to believe him. I leaned against the timbers' tarry, rough flanks for a long time in silence. I was watching the water, trying to see the exact place and the exact moment that it turned into crested waves, and the waves into white horses. I wanted to be ready.

CHAPTER THIRTEEN

On Thursday morning, I slept in and then lay on the front room carpet watching a fall fashion show on television. I was still feeling lazy after yesterday's trip to St. Ives, and my leg muscles were sore from fighting the surf. Skye, arriving home after a walk, glanced at me in surprise.

"Don't you have singing this morning?" she asked.

"Oh, shoot!" I glanced at my watch; my lesson started in ten minutes. I flapped shut the pages of my poetry book, in which I'd been writing during commercial breaks, and rushed to hide it in my closet where Skye wouldn't find it.

When I went out, the streets of Falmouth were crowded with pedestrians: art students with nose rings and green hair, fishermen-type guys in peaked caps and rubber boots, women shopping in the bakeries and greengrocers. I dodged between them all, then headed down a steep alley that funneled toward the harbor. I skipped down three sets of shallow, cobbled steps and then ducked into a doorway between a fish-and-chip shop and a second-hand bookstore. A flight of stairs led to the old sail loft where my singing teacher, Mrs. Pengelly, awaited me.

"Sorry if I'm late," I gasped, bursting in.

She moved across the room toward me in her serene manner, her wavy silver hair gleaming in the light reflected off the harbor water.

"Never mind," she said graciously. "Catch your breath."

I sat on the edge of one of her overstuffed floral chairs and ran my eyes over the portraits on the walls: dramatic shots of opera singers with mouths stretched open.

Mrs. Pengelly, seated at the baby grand piano, ran her fingers over the keyboard, producing rippling arpeggios while I panted inelegantly. Even when I wasn't panting, Mrs. Pengelly always made me feel inelegant, gangly as a colt. There was something just right about her heath-ery, tweedy skirts and lambswool sweaters and strings of pearls, her upright posture. Most of all, I liked her smile. When she smiled at me, I felt as if she genuinely liked me and wasn't teaching me just for the money.

"Have you practiced the aria we began last week?" she asked.

I shook my head. "No," I mumbled. "I've been — busy."

"I see." Turning from the piano, Mrs. Pengelly gave me a long, considering look. "Stella, do you mind if I ask why you're doing this?"

"Singing?"

"Yes."

Good question, but what was I going to answer? Should I say that I wanted to be a rock star or that I was trying to please my dead mother? Either answer seemed suddenly ridiculous.

"To be a singer requires dedication, sacrifices, endurance, and perseverance," said Mrs. Pengelly gently. "I'm not sure that you're serious about singing, Stella."

I flushed and chewed my lip. I'm a fake, I thought — the same thought I'd had while lying on the beach in St. Ives. Mrs. Pengelly has seen right through me and now she knows that inside me there's nothing except confusion.

"Singing for pleasure is perfectly commendable," said Mrs. Pengelly. "A trained voice can bring you pleasure all your life. But perhaps there's something else you might feel more serious about, more motivated by. What else do you enjoy doing?"

"I write," I blurted out. "Poems — and song lyrics." The words flashed away from me like swallows. I couldn't believe I was telling an adult this stuff. I couldn't believe the words had been there, so close to the surface of my mind without my ever noticing them.

Unlike me, Mrs. Pengelly didn't seem surprised by my answer. Her eyes were still calm and considering; no flicker of humor suggested that I might have said something foolish. "What else do you write?" she asked.

"Well, at school, I'm usually an A student in Language Arts," I said. "And in grade four, my teacher said on my report card that I 'have a way with words.' Then in grade six, I was excused from doing all the language exercises — you know, stuff like circling the verbs in sentences and giving the definitions for lists of nouns — and I was allowed to sit at the back of the class and write stories instead."

"Your teacher must have thought you had talent."

"I guess." I'd never considered this before. I had just been thankful to escape the boring exercises.

"And do you still write stories?"

"Right now, I'm mainly writing poems. While I'm on holiday, I mean. But last winter I wrote a novella and some short stories."

"Have you considered being a writer?"

"Not really," I said.

"Perhaps you should," said Mrs. Pengelly, sitting upright on her piano bench with her long fingers folded calmly on her tweed pleats. "Perhaps you should be taking writing classes instead of singing lessons."

I shrugged uncertainly. Would my mother have considered this a worthwhile career for me, my fingers clicking over a keyboard as I sat alone in a room? Writers weren't stars, were they? They were solitary people, people who lived in alternative realities and only appeared occasionally on dust jackets in boring black-and-white photographs. No one cared what they wore, how their bodies flowed when they walked, whether they were beautiful.

"You could study creative writing at university; you're

a bright student," said Mrs. Pengelly. "And there's journalism, too, of course."

I nodded, staring at the carpet with its controlled pattern of stiff flowers and leaves. Journalists didn't even appear on dust jackets. They were nothing but names that no one read, appearing in small print on newspaper pages that were tossed out every day or used to light fires or wrap fish and chips. Journalists risked their lives in jungles interviewing guerilla fighters; they were held hostage by bandits in mountain passes; they were shot in other people's wars. There was nothing romantic about journalism.

"Are you ready to sing?" Mrs. Pengelly asked kindly, and I nodded and moved over to stand closer to her gleaming piano. For the next thirty minutes, there was no time to think of anything other than notes and breathing, tempo, diminuendo and crescendo.

My lesson ended as the next student arrived at the door. "Good morning, Giles," Mrs. Pengelly said. She gathered up the sheets of music she'd been playing from and searched in the piano bench for what she needed next.

"I'll see you next Thursday at eleven, Stella," she said, giving me her calm smile. "And I hope you'll think about your writing."

"Yes," I said. "Goodbye."

I sneaked a quick, curious glance at Giles as I exited; Mrs. Pengelly had said he was a tenor of national fame, but I couldn't believe it. He didn't look anything like I imagined a singer of national fame would: he was short and stout, balding and red-faced, with thick, blunt fingers.

When he smiled at me, I saw his teeth were crooked. I thought he looked more like a farmer or someone who worked outside all day in the wind and sun. Not like someone who, according to Mrs. Pengelly, could "hold audiences in the palm of his hand."

I dawdled along the main street, stopping to look at neon-green sandals in the window of a shoe store, to admire a display of flowered T-shirts in a clothes store. I was aware of my mind dividing into two parts, one half working at converting the pounds on price tags into dollars, and the other half thinking about writing. *I'm a writer*, this half of my mind said, trying out the words. Did I like the sound of them? *I'm a poet.* I imagined the words tripping nonchalantly off my tongue at parties; how other people would respond with admiration or interest. I imagined myself dressed in black, looking mysterious and remote, appearing on television to discuss the central metaphor in my most recently published novel with an earnest host . . .

Barp, barp!

A small, snubnosed delivery truck negotiated the street, its gears grinding as it wheezed between parked vehicles and slowed for pedestrians crossing in front of it. I stepped into the doorway of a bakery, where cinnamon and chocolate smells wafted past my nose. Impulsively, I went inside to the glass counter and ordered two Florentines and two saffron buns for me and Nicholas, who was supposed to be coming over for lunch. Then I thought about Skye and changed my order of each goodie to three. Nicholas wouldn't like it if I left Skye out.

In the street again, I wondered which universities in Canada offered degrees in Creative Writing. I still felt amazed at the way in which the words "I write" had tumbled from my mouth in response to Mrs. Pengelly's question. How long had those words been lodged under my tongue, waiting for a chance to fly free? Why had I never before thought of being a writer? In grade six, my class had been visited by an author who wrote teen mysteries; I remembered how the other students crowded around after her presentation; how they wanted her to autograph copies of her books; how they tried to hold her interest with garbled plots from stories they'd written for the teacher. I had stood at the back, not interested in competing for her attention, not even thinking of showing her the stories I wrote at home in my room on long weekend afternoons. My writing was just something that was a part of me, like breathing and eating; it had never been something I thought about much, not something that could lead anywhere. It just was.

Reaching the library, I slipped inside and found a free computer station. After dropping my 50 pence into the plastic basket, I logged on. No e-mail from Ashley, but surprise! Noah had sent me one. How had he managed this from his wilderness camp?

Yo, Stella, what's happening over there? I'm using the Head Counselor's laptop. I've been hauling his share of supplies for a canoe trip all morning, and kissing his boots, to get this opportunity. He said I could have five minutes ONLY. Cheap, man! Cool laptop though — okay, so you don't want to hear

*about it. Stuff's cool here: blackflies the size of
Sikorsky helicopters, forest fires to the north (we've
watched the water bombers go over), and I've got
muscles like a voyageur from all the paddling.
Nearly ran into a moose yesterday around a bend
in the river. Listen up, Stella, you're keeping me
awake at night. I've been getting bad vibes about
you and all that salty blue water you're surrounded
by. Will you please not go on strangers' boats or
forget to learn the tide tables by heart? Say "No
thanks" when a pirate asks you on a date. I mean
it, you're out of your depth in salt water — it's deep
stuff. Yow!! This laptop guy just swiped me in the
neck and said I've had my five minutes. Back to
the portage trail.*

Love, Noah xxxxxxx

I printed a copy of Noah's e-mail and headed back outside. It was a strange message, I thought. Noah never
fussed or worried or did a big brother act on me. Once,
when we were eight, he'd told Dad that I was in trouble
and then ran to the farm's "back forty" and found me
stuck up a tree while a macho steer circled the base,
snorting and pawing. Noah, usually so mild and kind
with animals, threw rocks at it until it galloped away.
When Dad asked him later how he knew I'd needed help,
he shrugged and said, "I just knew."

So what did Noah "just know" right now that I didn't?
Or was he merely feeling spooked because we'd never
been this far apart before? Or had the blackflies poi-
soned his bloodstream and messed up his brain? At least

he was thinking about me, which was more than I'd been doing about him. Being so far from home and experiencing so many new things seemed to have taken up all my mental energy. For a moment, waiting to cross the street, I closed my eyes and focused on Noah. Heat crept through me, the smell of balsam fir, the splash of a paddle in clear water. Noah's laughter echoed over the water, then faded as the traffic grumbled to a halt and the pedestrians around me stepped into the road. I hurried across the street.

Everything was okay with Noah, I thought. Except for his unease regarding me.

"Hey," said Nicholas. "Earth to Stella."

"What? Oh!" I saw that I had already reached the old warehouse and had almost walked past Nicholas without noticing him as he leaned against a lamppost near the entrance.

"I was thinking," I said, trying for some of Mrs. Pengelly's unruffled dignity.

"Sounds dangerous," said Nicholas. "You'll short-circuit your motherboard."

"Very funny," I complained, climbing the stairs ahead of him.

"We're home!" I called, swinging open the apartment door. It was a relief not to worry about Skye's mess, not to care. I knew now that none of it mattered to Nicholas. He thought Skye was wonderful.

We dropped our bags just inside the door and then Nicholas brushed past me, heading toward Skye's corner of the living room like a hound dog tracking. I wandered after him.

"Have a good morning?" Skye asked, turning to greet us. There were fresh smears of paint on her shirt, and even some clinging to strands of her hair. Her big new canvas was already covered in paint, although she'd just started work on it yesterday. She must have been painting the whole time Nicholas and I were in St. Ives, and perhaps late into the night too.

"The morning was fine," I replied, but Nicholas was silent, rummaging in his backpack. When he stood up, he held out his sketchpad. "Would you like to see my work?" he asked Skye. "It's just sketches and small colored stuff. My big pieces are at home, at my mom's."

Skye took the sketchpad and leafed slowly through it as I peered over her shoulder. Nicholas' work was good; even I could tell that. Little fishing boats bobbed on the waves with just the right lines on their hulls; our seal pup stared at us with round eyes and just the right expression of helplessness. And surprise! There was a sketch of me, staring out of the train window on the way to St. Ives. There were watercolors, too, with aquamarine sea and bright flowers against yellow cottage walls.

"These are very good, excellent," Skye said warmly. "Your use of light and shadow is well executed, and you know how to use negative space to good effect. You have a fine, observant eye for line and shape."

Nicholas flushed in delight as Skye handed the pad back to him, and then he looked around her shoulder to where her own huge canvas was propped on the easel.

"What's this new one called?" he asked.

"*Searching for El Dorado*," she replied.

As usual, it took me several minutes to figure out what

all the interwoven, overlapping, and mixed-together, semi-abstract shapes were. First of all, I figured out there were a lot of women on the canvas. They were all filing along snaking paths that looped up and down hills, crossing and intersecting like the walkways in a maze. The paths were surrounded by trees with graceful branches, and masses of tropical-looking flowers, and leaves in many different shapes. However, none of the women could see any of this surrounding beauty because they were all wearing blinkers on their faces, like the blinkers racehorses wear so they can only see straight ahead.

What lay ahead of every woman, at the end of her long path, was a place that Skye had painted in golden: golden walls, golden cobblestones. In the middle of all the gold were —

"Did you cut up my magazines?" I asked in horror. I fixed Skye with an accusing glare.

"No," she said evenly. "I bought my own."

"Oh." I went back to studying the golden spaces in the painting. They were filled with pieces of photos cut from magazines and scrambled up to form a collage: a pair of perfect legs, one closed eye with black curling lashes (an ad for mascara), the grill of a BMW, a bottle of perfume, lips wearing pearly pink lipstick, an executive briefcase, a pair of shoes by Armani, Cartier earrings, the window of a house with stained glass and flowers. Lines of golden paint surrounded, crossed, and linked the collage pieces.

All the blinkered women on the paths were pointing at the golden spaces as they struggled along.

"It's symbolic again," said Nicholas.

"What do you think it means?" Skye asked.

Get ready for a lecture, I thought. Does she think we're morons? I yawned and headed for the kitchen, opening the fridge door and rustling foil wrap on some leftover meat. But I could still hear the conversation in the living room.

"Well, it might be about capitalism," Nicholas ventured.

"Yes, okay," Skye agreed.

"Like, the Spanish were always trying to find a city of gold and now people are looking for all this material stuff. Obsessed with getting it."

"Yes, the perfect life, the happy ending that they can buy," agreed Skye. "That's what ads tell us. If we buy the right stuff, we will be fit, healthy, and have perfect lives. But marketing isn't about happiness. It's about the people at the top making money off everyone else. So if companies can convince women that they need all these products to be acceptable people, to be beautiful and successful, they can make a bundle off the women."

"You got the idea from that same program, the Atlantis program?" asked Nicholas.

"Yes," Skye admitted. "I came to Cornwall to paint cliffs and sea — but I seem to keep going off on tangents." She laughed.

I bit off a mouthful of cold roast and chewed in silence, staring at the closed fridge door. Going off on tangents. Yeah, right. Trying to lecture Stella was more like it. Trying to convert me to Skye's World View. Going on like some sort of a teacher, so wise and so clever. Well, she needn't think I was going to sit in the front row of her lecture circuit and hang onto her words. I took another bite from the slice of beef and wandered to my room.

The bed sagged under me. I kicked off my thongs and rested my bare feet on the fuzzy coverlet and stared at the picture of my mother on the bedside table. What would she have said to Skye? There was a magazine lying by the picture and I began to flip through it, searching for anything I hadn't read yet. But the photos kept snagging my eyes. Was it true, really, truly true, that nothing but profit margins and quarterly financial reports lay behind the glossy pictures? Was it true that a picture could lie? Was it true that models did not live happily ever after? Skye could be right, a tiny voice suggested in my head. Selling is about making money, not about helping people live their lives.

Even if this was true, when I stared at the pictures I couldn't help what happened: all I felt was the tug and pull of desire, a longing to be as leggy, wide eyed, smoothly beautiful, and gorgeously dressed as the models.

Of course, said the voice in my head. If the ads didn't make you want, they wouldn't be working. Skye's right; it's only about selling stuff. About wanting.

My mother smiled at me from her frame and a hot wave of guilt washed through me. It felt disloyal even to hear that cold, hard voice of reason in my head. If Skye was right, did that make my mother wrong?

I flung the magazine onto the floor in disgust and wandered back into the front room. Maybe by now the lecture would be over. Besides, I wanted another slice of roast beef.

"Nicholas and I are having soup," Skye said to me from the small kitchen, which was separated from the front room by a counter island. "Would you like some?"

"Yes, please. And I've brought some buns and Florentines for dessert."

Soon we were seated around the table, our bowls of soup resting in the spaces we'd cleared amongst cut-up magazines, scraps of discarded paper, paintbrushes, and paint rags.

"Did you paint all of yesterday while we were in St. Ives?" Nicholas asked, and I rolled my eyes and blew on a spoonful of soup. Did he have to be so interested in Skye?

"Yes, most of the day," she replied. "I was too excited about the picture to leave it for my art class. Though I took a walk through town around lunchtime. Almost spent my 'mad money,'" she said, glancing at me with a glimmer in her eyes. She must've known I was sick of hearing about her "mad money."

"I almost bought a lamp made from a sea urchin shell," she continued. "But then I figured I'd never get it home unbroken. The shell had stripes of lovely colors on it."

"People around here dive for them, bring them up, and clean the spines off," Nicholas explained.

"I've got some news for you, Stella," Skye said, changing the subject. "There's a wonderful exhibition on in London, the work of a woman called Lucy Collins. My art class is planning to go up this weekend; our instructor has been promised a group rate for accommodations and the entrance fee. It's a great opportunity and I'd really love to go."

"What about me?" I asked. "Do I have to come?"

"I thought that you'd probably be bored," she replied. "I've talked to Richard, and asked if you could spend the weekend at Rose Mullion. He said that would be fine. I've talked to your dad, too, and he agrees with the plan."

"You talked to Dad?" I asked. "When? How come I didn't get to talk to him?"

"You hadn't come home yet from St. Ives when I called him. But you can talk to him tonight if you like," Skye responded reasonably. Trying to make up for the fact that she'd been having a cozy chat with Dad while I was out. Like he belonged to her more than to me. I bent my face over my soup and stirred it around, watching pieces of celery and rice swirl past the tip of my spoon, swallowing past the disappointed lump in my throat.

"I'll be leaving Friday evening, that's tomorrow, on the night train to London," Skye continued. "I'll be back on Monday for our last week in Cornwall."

I started to focus on what she was saying, instead of whining to myself about missing a call to Dad. This could be fun, I realized. A whole weekend without Skye, for Nicholas and me to spend as we chose.

"Cool," Nicholas and I said simultaneously.

CHAPTER FOURTEEN

"We're going camping," Nicholas said shortly, as if the words were being squeezed out between his teeth.

"We are?" I asked in surprise. "Where?"

"On the headland."

I followed the line of his gesturing arm and stared across the field dotted with Guernsey cows toward the rough track leading over the headland, the track I'd bounced over with the seal ladies. The headland looked soft in the still evening air, the low golden light. But I knew there was nothing soft about it; it was hard with granite and quartz, prickly with heather and furze. It fell abruptly away into cold wind and dizzying space, into the sea. A chill trickled through me.

I turned my attention back to Nicholas. He was surrounded by stuff strewn on the gravel of Rose Mullion's driveway: tarps and bright tent fabric, yellow plastic pegs, pieces of white nylon rope, a hammer, a flashlight.

"Is this okay with your dad?" I asked as he began stuffing things into a green pack.

"How the hell should I know?" he snarled.

"What's the matter?"

He didn't answer, just went on stuffing things into his pack: a paperback book, a bag of peanuts. His dark hair fell forward over his face, hiding it from me. His long, thin fingers gripped stuff too tightly; I saw his pale knuckles on the spine of the book.

"I thought we were going to a movie," I complained, smoothing my own fingers over the dress I'd bought that afternoon in Falmouth, playing with the string of heartshaped beads around my throat.

"You'll have to get changed," Nicholas replied. "We're not going to the flicks."

"Why not?"

"Because my dad went and forgot, didn't he? He said —" and here Nicholas began to mimic Richard's voice, "'Oh, by the way, Nicholas, I'm going to an auction tonight. Estate sale in Exeter, beautiful stuff. Can't miss it.'"

I glanced around. The silver car and the white truck were both absent from their usual parking spots.

"What did you say?" I asked.

"I reminded him that you were coming for the weekend

and that he'd promised to take us out for crab and a
movie."

"Then what?" I asked, moving my foot as a rope
trailed across it. Nicholas began folding up a tarp, wrapping the rope into the folds.

"He said he couldn't miss the sale, and he was sure
we'd find something else to do. Like he could care less
what I do with my life." Nicholas knotted the end of the
rope around the bundled tarp, tightened it with an angry
jerk, and slung it down by his pack.

"So why are we camping?" I asked.

"Because I don't feel like sleeping in his house." More
words squeezed between teeth.

"Okay," I said with a resigned sigh. Leaving Nicholas,
I trailed into Rose Mullion with my pack slung over one
shoulder. The weekend without Skye was getting off to a
fab start! And what would Skye think if she knew that
Richard was not even home tonight, that Nicholas and
I were alone on the cliffs? Should I call her and tell her? I
glanced at my watch. Six ten. She'd be en route to London
already; she was catching a train in Falmouth at five-
thirty and having dinner with the rest of her art group in
Truro before they went north overnight. I could call Dad,
but what could he do? Canada seemed far away, another
world: a soft, familiar place where my father sat in his
study in the humid evening air and couldn't begin to
imagine the chill grandeur of the Cornish cliffs around
Rose Mullion. A call from me would only worry him.

I was on my own.

My footsteps slapped hollowly on the hall tiles, and
the house echoed them back from its empty, silent spaces.

In a washroom that said "W.C." on the door and contained a pedestal basin and an antique tub with claw feet, I shrugged out of my dress. Rummaging in my pack, I found a pair of jeans and a sweater and changed into them. Using cotton pads, I cleaned off my mascara (no point looking like a raccoon after a night in a tent) and then smiled into the mirror as I heard the approaching click of Blondie's toenails. She whined softly outside the door. I swung it open and stroked the smooth muzzle that she poked toward me.

"Good girl," I crooned, feeling as if I'd found an ally. I'd take her camping.

Blondie followed me down the hall as I left. Just as I approached the door to go back outside, there was a noise behind me. A sigh, something moving across the floor. Hair rose on my neck. I swung on my heels. The house was empty, wasn't it? At the far end of the hall, a door stood open a crack. In the space between door and frame, the anxious face of the foreign woman peered out.

"Hi, there!" I said, my voice too loud with nervousness, my words bouncing down the hall toward the woman like rubber balls. She didn't reply and swung the door shut so suddenly that I blinked. Had I imagined her? She was weird; she gave me the creeps. At least Peter wasn't around; he gave me the creeps, too. I never knew whether he'd smile and call me love or whether he'd be ranting about foreigners and the price of petrol and taxes paid to the English.

I hurried outside into the low sunlight with Blondie pressed warm and silky against my legs. "I'm ready," I told Nicholas. "And I'm starving. Can we eat before we go?"

"I've packed some food," he said, knotting rope around a bundle of kindling with quick skill. "We'll have a fire in the cove."

In my absence, he had filled two large packs that bulged at his feet like overweight grubs. Each had a roll of foam mattress snugged across the bottom. Beside each pack lay a tent bag that we'd obviously have to carry.

"Ready?" Nicholas asked, lifting a pack and swinging it to me. I shrugged into it, its weight settling onto me, hanging from my shoulders, squeezing the blood from my spine.

"Sheesh, what's in this thing?" I asked rebelliously.

Maybe I wouldn't go; I'd just catch the bus back to town and watch music videos and eat junk food and pretend Skye didn't live in the apartment at all. This camping idea was dumb. Then I remembered how Nicholas had held my hand in St. Ives, when I was feeling down about my mother, and I noticed how pinched and tight his mouth looked as he swung his own pack over the shoulders of his black leather jacket. I knew that there was hurt lying beneath his anger, waiting its turn to emerge. If I was his friend, I wouldn't abandon him now.

With a whistle to Blondie, I headed toward the stile and swung myself over it, my knees protesting beneath the weight of my pack. The three of us crossed the field in silence while cows watched us with their dark round eyes. Yellow flies buzzed over cow pats, and the sound of the sea below the cliffs rose up to us as a soft hush, like breathing. At the far side of the field, we climbed another granite stile, its wide slabs hoary with lichen.

"I thought we'd camp here," Nicholas said.

I looked around, pleased we were not going onto the open cliffs. At my back, the hedge surrounding the cow's field was a solid bulk of grass and flowers topped with the occasional May tree stunted and twisted by the prevailing westerly wind. We searched beneath the hedge for level spots, and then we laid tarps over the rabbit-bitten turf. I hauled my tent from its bag and spread it over the tarp, trying to figure it out.

"Hold this," Nicholas instructed, handing me a pole that he'd assembled. He tweaked the tent into shape, then showed me the sleeves to thread the poles through. Once the small blue tent was up, we banged in pegs with a stone. I crawled inside and unrolled the thin foam pad and covered it with the sleeping bag I'd found in my pack. Nicholas' tent was standing now, an equally small green dome. I glanced around at the sweeping cliffs, the long line of blue sea against the sky. Huge ivory clouds, stained with gold, boiled up from the horizon, and a cool wind whispered over the rough ground and fingered my hair while the sea boomed far below. The tents looked small and fragile.

"Now what?" I asked uncertainly.

"Grub," Nicholas replied, lifting the bundle of kindling. "Bring your pack, it's got the sausages."

As we took the track, our long violet shadows slid ahead of us. A seagull slipstreamed up the cliff and into the sky on an updraft, and, far out, a white sail caught the last light and burst into brilliance like a petal. Maybe it was crossing to France. Maybe it was Richard.

"When did your dad leave?" I asked, before I remembered that he'd been heading for a sale in Exeter.

"After lunch," Nicholas replied. "I phoned to let you know but you were out."

We passed the spot where Nicholas had been hauled up the cliff by the Coastguard, and continued on for half a mile before branching off the track onto a thin path. Bracken brushed against my legs. The path crawled down the cliff into a small cove, twisting beneath my feet.

"Where's the tide?" I asked anxiously.

"Dropping."

Pebbles grated beneath our feet as we crossed the beach. When we reached a flat boulder, Nicholas slid his pack onto it and cut the rope around the kindling with a pocketknife. He crumpled newspaper, built a teepee of sticks over it, and added dry seaweed. Soon flames leaped up, bright against the darkening purple sea. We sat on the flat boulder and whittled sticks into points, then speared the sausages on them and let them drip fat into the fire as they cooked. Afterward, we ate peanuts, slices of cake, a chocolate bar, and a bag of chips that Nicholas called crisps. We threw food to Blondie, lying below the rock, and she gobbled it and sniffed around hopefully for crumbs.

The cove brimmed with silence, even though the waves whooshed on the sand with soft sighs and the embers of the fire crackled and snapped. The silence was ancient, bigger than the waves or the fire. It was filled with empty space and cold air and wind and stories I would never know.

I shivered and pulled my windbreaker over my sweater as the velvety darkness blended beach and sea and sky into one shade. Nicholas moved beside me on the boulder, rasping a match into flame. I shot him a startled glance.

"What are you doing?" I asked.

"What does it look like? Want one?"

"You've got to be kidding."

The smoke from his cigarette drifted past me, a harsh, alien smell in this place of salt and oxygen. I heard the sound of his lips, the sigh as he exhaled. His face gleamed faintly in the tip's glow, hard planes of cheek and jaw. He looked like a stranger.

I wrapped my arms around my knees and drew my chin into the collar of my windbreaker. I thought about my dad, the smell of books in his office, his smile. Maybe I should have called him. A worm of guilt twisted in my stomach. What was I doing here, on this dark shore with a stranger, with the menacing whisper of the black sea?

"So when did you start?" I asked.

There was a pause as Nicholas blew out smoke. "Last night," he replied.

"What for?"

"I felt like it," Nicholas said sullenly. "I was mad at my dad. I'm still mad. You think he's so great, Stella, but you don't know anything. You think you've got problems with Skye, but Skye's easy to live with, man. You're lucky and you don't even know it. You don't know what my dad's like to live with."

"So tell me."

Nicholas exhaled again and I buried my nose in my collar until the smoke had drifted past. Irritation flickered in me but I tried to ignore it. "Tell me," I repeated.

"He doesn't care about anything," Nicholas began. "Don't you see that? He doesn't care that Skye thinks you're staying safely at Rose Mullion tonight. He never cared when he upset my mom. He's never cared about anything except getting his own way and getting money."

Somewhere, high in the dark sky, curlews flew over crying. Their thin, sharp voices trickled down my back like cold water. The tip of Nicholas' cigarette glowed as he dragged on it.

"Money, money, money," he repeated bitterly. "He's too cheap to send my mother any. He's too cheap to pay my train fare to Cornwall. And meanwhile he's driving a sports car and picking up blondes in pubs and sailing around in a mucky great yacht. Last year, I won a trip to the London galleries in an art contest. I needed to have a parent come with me, but he wouldn't come. So I couldn't go, because my mom's boss wouldn't give her the time off. You know what he said when my mother called this summer to arrange my trip down here?"

I shook my head and waited while Nicholas smoked.

"He asked if there wasn't anywhere else she could send me to. Like thanks, Dad. It's great to feel so wanted. And then, when you arrived, he was so happy because it meant he could go on ignoring me and I'd still have things to do. You could keep me out of his hair."

"But he paid for stuff for us," I argued. "Horse riding and the theme park and stuff."

"You think that replaces spending time with someone?" Nicholas asked scornfully. "You think it's better to hand someone a ten-quid note so they can get lost, or to say you'll go with them?"

"He took us sailing," I said stubbornly.

"He was taking the boat out anyway, to play with the new genoa. He wasn't doing us a big favor."

Nicholas flung his butt away and it died in a rock pool with a sizzle.

"And this weekend? He promised he'd be around and we could do some stuff together," Nicholas said. "He promised," he repeated, and there was a broken sound about his voice.

Promised, promised . . . the word seemed to fill the cove, mocking us as it bounced back and forth.

I reached out and laid my palm flat over Nicholas' hand on the rock.

"He's never cared enough to worry," Nicholas said. "When my mother left him? He didn't even ask whether I was going too."

I felt Nicholas' hand twitch under mine, and I wished I knew what to say. My tongue seemed stuck to the roof of my mouth. After a moment, Nicholas pulled his hand away from my silence and another match rasped as he lit up. The cigarette tip glowed into life.

Two wrongs don't make a right, Pearl had told me on more than one occasion. I tried to think of a different way to say the same thing. "Hurting yourself doesn't make your dad care any more," I said. "If he's never cared, he won't start just because you're smoking."

"I'm not doing it for him."

"Why then?"

Nicholas gave an irritated shrug. "Just felt like it," he muttered. "What does anything matter?"

"Well, you matter to me," I said bravely. "And you

matter to your mother. And you're going to be a name on book spines whether your dad cares about it or not. Remember?"

Nicholas shrugged again, a sulky twitch under black leather. Suddenly, I knew exactly what to tell him; Skye had given me the words like a gift.

"Remember, when you showed Skye your work, she said it was really good. Later, she told me you'll get into art school with no problem, that your paintings are full of promise."

"She said that?" Nicholas asked.

"Yes. Full of promise," I repeated.

We sat in silence for a moment, and I wondered if I should say any more. I decided to go for it. "And smoking matters," I said firmly. "Smoking's only for dummies, Nicholas. You're not a dummy."

We sat in silence for a long time after that. Nicholas finished his cigarette. The lights of a tanker passed slowly up the channel, far out. Once, a bird cried on the cliffs. The flat rock seemed to grow colder and colder under me, and pins and needles prickled in my legs. The last embers glowed orange on the beach, where our fire had been, and the waves hissed on the sand.

I stood up stiffly at last. "I'm tired," I said. "Let's go now."

Nicholas sighed, as if he was coming back from some other place, and stood up beside me. The beam of his flashlight swung across the shingle, searching through the dark for the start of the path, the way a dog's nose searches for a smell in the grass. Blondie yawned and trotted after us.

At the top of the cliff, we found the rough track between the bracken and furze. The full moon had risen now, and we didn't need the flashlight. The moon filled the sky with a soft, radiant glow and shimmered a path of fish scales across the black sea from the horizon to the foot of the cliffs.

"Look how beautiful it is," I said, pausing, turning eastward. "You could paint it."

A wind whispered through my hair, through the bracken, and I shivered inside my jacket. We walked on along the track side by side, heading for our small tents in the hedge's shelter.

Nicholas reached for my hand. "Thanks, Stella," he said softly into the dark, giving my fingers a friendly squeeze. Hope warmed me, filling the hollow place created in me by the night wind and the black sea. Perhaps I had said something right, words like the gift of a white horse.

CHAPTER FIFTEEN

The first thing I noticed when I awoke was the dampness. The sleeping bag seemed glued to me with moisture and even my bones felt chilled. I pulled the tent flap open and peered into a wooly, gray world.

"Aargh," came from Nicholas' tent.

"What's the matter?"

"Even my fags are damp."

"Good," I said unsympathetically. "Cigarettes are even grosser when they're damp."

I glared at my jeans. Damp denim was totally gross, too, I thought as I pulled the jeans on gingerly before climbing outside. We might have been anywhere. The thick sea mist had blotted everything out — the world was wrapped in cotton wool that wisped coldly against my cheeks. Nicholas struggled from his tent to stand beside me.

"You're looking a bit green," I said, staring at his pale cheeks.

He grunted and glared at the tents. "They always did leak," he said in disgust. "Even when I was a kid. Even in this mizzle. What time is it?"

"Five fifty-five," I replied, squinting at my watch in the dull pewter light.

"I'm hungry," Nicholas grumbled.

"So, let's head home for breakfast and some dry clothes. We can't crawl back into wet tents."

Blondie appeared suddenly from the mist, her silky coat dark with water and a spider web draped over her back. She stuck her nose into my hand. "Where have you been?" I asked.

"She hogged my sleeping bag all night," said Nicholas, giving her back a fond pat. "Then she went out exploring."

I slung my pack over my shoulder and headed for the stile. The tents could wait until later. The field was a soup cauldron of mist; the cows were invisible although we could hear their teeth wrenching grass.

"Let's follow the hedge instead of cutting across the middle of the field," I suggested. The mist made me feel disoriented, as if I was caught in that state between waking and dreaming. I could almost believe that I might walk into the middle of the field and lose myself, never make it out the other side.

So we followed the hedge, moving cautiously forward through the mist. Somewhere to our left a foghorn moaned a low, monotonous warning.

"Here, if we climb over here we'll come out in the garden," said Nicholas. He stuck his boot into the grass and brambles on the hedge and hauled himself to the top. In a moment he disappeared, as though the mist had swallowed him whole. I scrambled my way to the top, paused to eat three ripe blackberries, and then dropped down beside him, amongst the rhododendron bushes below Rose Mullion. Blondie whined behind us.

"Don't worry, she'll run around and —" Nicholas started to say.

I grabbed his arm and jerked. "Sshh. Listen. Who is it?"

After a moment, Nicholas set his pack on the ground, dropped to his hands, and began to move forward through the mist and thick shrubbery like a gorilla. I followed his example, straining my ears. I was positive I'd heard voices, but wasn't Richard away? Could it be the strange woman talking to someone else? But who else would be in the yard at this hour of the morning? Ahead of me, Nicholas dropped suddenly onto his stomach and waved his hand at me. I dropped, too, and then wriggled forward to lie beside him. Ahead, I could catch glimpses of gravel through the dark leaves and low-hanging branches of the rhododendron that arched over us. Legs moved through my line of vision: a pair of jeans ending in rubber sea boots.

"Peter!" hissed Nicholas into my ear. He began to wriggle farther forward but I grabbed him by the belt and hauled on him; he might give us away with the sound of dead leaves shuffling beneath his belly. Lucky that everything was impregnated with dampness; the dead leaves were soggy instead of brittle and dry.

Beyond Peter's legs, I thought I saw tires and patches of white. Was the antiques truck in the yard? There was the squeak and whisper of a door opening — the side door of the house. I recognized its sound.

"Ere we are then, love," said Peter's voice, jolly and surprisingly loud. "Better late than never, as me gran used to say."

I flinched and crouched lower against the ground, the smell of wet earth and green moss filling my nose.

Suddenly, there was a jostle of movement in the yard: the worn brown leather shoes of a woman moving across the gravel from the direction of the door, and two new pairs of legs in gray pants. Men's pants. The feet and legs jostled around close together as though their owners were standing very close. I raised myself on my elbows and was able to see more.

"It's her," I breathed to Nicholas and he nodded, propped on his elbows beside me. The foreign woman from Rose Mullion, the woman we were so puzzled about, was hugging two shabbily dressed men. There was something fierce about the way she hugged them, as if she'd been afraid she'd never see them again, and she wiped her hands across her face as she stepped away. One of the men was dark and straight, but the other was older and bent, with gray hair. Both had worn faces that looked almost yellow in the dim light.

There was a clanking noise, which sounded like the truck's rear door being opened. A stick dug into my elbow and I crawled forward carefully. But Nicholas shot me a warning look, so I dropped onto my stomach again. Now all I could see was feet.

"'Ere ee go then," said Peter, his boots striding across my line of vision.

The other legs moved away toward the truck, and I caught foreign words being exchanged quietly between the woman and the two men. The feet all disappeared.

"What's happening?" I breathed at Nicholas, and he wriggled a little farther forward. I waited, lying still, hearing the foghorn out at sea and noticing a piece of bark tangled in Nicholas' hair.

"They're giving Peter money," Nicholas hissed in my ear. "He's counting through a wad of bills."

Suddenly, Nicholas dropped flat and lay like a stone. Blondie's paws scampered across the yard.

She'll smell us, I thought in panic. She'll come bouncing in here and give us away. I tried to hold my breath, my face pressed on the ground, not a muscle twitching. I could almost feel Peter's dark gaze tunneling through the bushes like x-rays, boring a hole in the back of my pale, exposed neck. I remembered the contemptuous way he spat words between his teeth, the size of his biceps, the black hair at his wrists, the scornful stare of his mermaid tattoo. My skin crawled.

"Get away, go on," I heard Peter's voice and then the slam of the truck's rear door, gravel crunching, the slam of the cab door, the roar of the motor starting. After a moment, the vehicle moved, and soon it was growing quieter, moving away up the lane toward the road.

A long sigh slipped out between my lips and I raised

my head a couple of inches from the dirt, noticing the ache in my hips. Blondie arrived in a flurry of wet hair and dark leaves and snapping twigs, whining happily at finding us. Nicholas sat up cautiously and laid a hand on her muzzle. We waited. Water dripped from the leaves. The foghorn moaned. A snail crawled in front of me, waving its horns and leaving a shining trail.

"Okay?" I whispered, sitting up and pulling leaves from my hair.

We crawled out and crossed the yard to the house, kicking off wet shoes inside the door and trailing the wet hems of our jeans along the tiles into the kitchen.

"What was all that about?" I asked. I could feel my eyes, stretched wide.

"Peter took the woman and the two men in the back of the lorry," Nicholas said tensely. He looked even paler than he had when we awoke. "He's running a pipeline."

"What?"

"He's using my father's lorry to run refugees around. Think back to what he said before."

"He said to the woman . . . four days and he'd take her upcountry with her old man and her dad," I said. "And that was on Tuesday. Right?"

"Right. So that was who the two men were. And she's been waiting for them to arrive."

"But where would they come from?" I asked, peeling off wet socks and then getting out bread to make toast. "I mean, did they just arrive from some other part of the country?"

"We're at the end of the country," said Nicholas patiently. "They must have arrived by boat. Across the channel. Someone brought them over and then Peter picked them up with the van, brought them here to collect the woman, and then headed upcountry with them."

"We should tell your dad," I said. "When does he get back from Exeter?"

Nicholas looked momentarily sullen and shrugged. "Dunno. He doesn't give me a copy of his schedule," he said sarcastically.

It was while I was slicing bread that I realized it.

I looked at Nicholas. He gave me a level look and I knew that he'd realized it, too. If the woman had used Richard's house to wait in, then Richard didn't need us to tell him about Peter's pipeline. Richard must know about it.

"Maybe he gets a cut," Nicholas said. "For letting Peter use the lorry."

"The secret compartment," I said.

"Right."

I jumped when the toast popped up, even though I'd been staring at the toaster.

"Very convenient," Nicholas said consideringly. "Peter's driving all over the place, delivering furniture anyway, so why not make a few extra quid on the side? The refugees can hop out in London or Liverpool or some place, in an alley when no one is looking."

"Wouldn't driving them around be a criminal offense?" I asked.

Nicholas nodded, munching toast smeared with strawberry jam.

What about being an accomplice — isn't that a criminal offense, too? I wanted to ask. But after a glance at

Nicholas' pale jaw line, I took another bite of toast instead. We chewed in silence.

"I'm going back to bed," Nicholas said when his toast was finished.

"Me too."

We were halfway down the hall leading to the bedroom wing when the side door whispered open again. We both froze. Was Peter back? Would he walk in without knocking?

Footsteps approached down the entrance hall.

Richard gazed at us. Something like shock flickered in his eyes. "What the devil are you doing up so early?" he demanded.

"We camped out last night," I explained.

"Oh. Just come home?"

"Yeah, just came home. Five minutes ago," lied Nicholas. I suppressed my flicker of surprise, held myself rigid, stared at my fingers. Had we left toast crumbs on the kitchen counter?

"When did you get back from Exeter?" Nicholas asked.

"Oh, last night, very late," Richard said without hesitation. "Assumed you were both asleep in bed."

"Up early, aren't you?" asked Nicholas coolly.

Bright spots of color burned in Richard's lean, brown face. Was he angry or embarrassed? I noticed his clothes: his rubber boots, his peaked sailing cap, the navy blue scarf knotted around his throat. Then he laughed easily, his teeth gleaming. "I've just been down in the cove to check *Fetha*'s anchor," he explained. "Couldn't sleep so thought I might as well get up. The barometer's been a bit unsteady."

Nicholas and I both stared at him assessingly; I noticed details, like the wet grass stuck to the toe of a boot. If he'd been down in the cove, did he know about Peter taking the woman away?

He grinned at us jauntily. "Cat got your tongues?" he asked. "I'm off to have some breakfast."

We didn't move until his footsteps died away down the tiled hall, then we went silently to our respective rooms. I pulled off my wet jeans and crashed in the guest-room bed. When I awoke, the sun was hanging in the mist like a white ball, casting a strange light over everything. I found Nicholas outside, throwing a stick for Blondie.

"Mist's burning off," he said. "Let's go and air out the tents."

We walked back across the field and hauled out the damp sleeping bags, laying them to dry on the heather. Nicholas was right: the mist was evaporating around us, headlands and blue sea creeping out of it, revealing themselves. If we wanted to use the tents again, they'd be dried out, ready for us. For lunch, we picked blackberries in the lane and ate them with sugar and cream. They leaked purple juice into the cream like dye. In the evening, we caught the bus to Falmouth and went to a movie. Richard picked us up afterward and drove us home; he didn't say anything about the movie we'd missed on Friday night due to his absence or about the crab dinner we'd been promised. I didn't know whether Nicholas was still upset or not, but we slept in the house because we were too tired to bother walking to the headland.

We didn't mention anything about smuggling.

On Sunday, we hung out in the cove, swimming and lying on the rocks, eating sandwiches and cookies (which Nicholas called biscuits), reading books, dabbling in rock pools. Nicholas painted a picture of shells and a red sea anemone. I wrote a poem about beach fires. We didn't see Peter or talk about smuggling. We only saw Richard when he came down to the cove and spent half an hour messing around on *Fetha*, coiling lines and folding sails and whatever else sailors do on their boats. Nicholas sat on a rock and smoked one of his Woodbines but Richard didn't say anything about it and neither did I. I just gave him my *Tomb Raider* glare.

It was a long, slow, hot day with nothing happening. I wrote postcards home and got a sunburned back. In the evening, Nicholas and I played blackjack and twenty-one until after midnight. I finally crawled into bed feeling relaxed in every muscle, and salty and warm.

On Monday morning, Nicholas lost a filling at breakfast.

"Youch!" he exclaimed, spitting out a disgusting mixture of toast and pieces of filling. He poked his tongue around in his mouth, wincing. "Lost the whole thing," he said gloomily.

"Does it hurt?" I asked.

"Yes."

"Better call Dr. Embury — that was who you used to see, wasn't it? He's in Truro now," said Richard, who was frying bacon and eggs.

Nicholas made the call as we listened. "Today?" he asked. "Three? Alright." He hung up the phone and shrugged at me apologetically. "I'll have to go," he said. "This flipping tooth is killing me."

"I'll give you a ride up to Truro about one," Richard offered. "I want to drop into the shop. Then you can catch the train back after your appointment."

After breakfast, Nicholas and I spent the morning in the garden reading books. We ate a quick lunch of sandwiches in the kitchen. After lunch, it was time for Nicholas to leave.

"Will you be here when I get back from Truro?" he asked as we followed Richard out to the car.

"Dunno," I replied. "Skye's getting home today. I might take the bus into Falmouth before you get back."

"I'll call you," he promised, climbing into the passenger seat.

"Good luck with your tooth!" I yelled after him, and he stuck an arm into the air and waved. Richard tooted the horn, and the silver car slid around a bend in the lane and out of sight.

It was very quiet. I wandered down to the cove, brushing past the orange montbretia flowers, nibbling the occasional ripe blackberry. For a long time I lay on the rocks, drowsy and hot. I wondered what the time was but I'd forgotten my watch in my pack in the spare bedroom. I felt too lazy to go back to Falmouth yet; besides, I didn't think that Skye would arrive home until late in the evening. Maybe I would wait for Nicholas and we could have a last swim before I headed back. Or maybe I would swim now. I sat up, gazing at the bright blue sea filling the cove. There was barely even a swell, the water nibbled on the sand as if too lazy to ripple into foam.

Never swim alone, said Dad's voice in my head. Promise? I had promised, but that was a long time ago, when I was a little kid. It wouldn't matter to take just a small dip, just a wade around. *I'm getting bad vibes about you and all that salty blue water*, Noah had e-mailed me. I tried to conjure up an image of the cove during the storm: all tossing waves and wind. But it seemed long ago, like something that had happened in another place. What could possibly happen today, on this calm, sleepy afternoon? Anyway, Nicholas would arrive soon.

I padded along the beach, wincing when a pebble jabbed into the sole of one foot. In the boathouse, I took Nicholas' wet suit from the rafters and pulled it on over my bikini, careful that my fingernails didn't puncture the black neoprene. The suit was not a perfect fit but it was good enough. At the water's edge, I pulled on my mask and snorkel then slid my toes into the clear water, watching them shimmer and grope their way out between the rocks. Silently, I slipped into deeper water. It was aqua green, shading to indigo blue around the rocks.

White sand glimmered eight feet below my drifting body. A flat fish undulated across the bottom; a small crab scuttled away from it, while a sharper-nosed fish flashed past my arm. I floated, unmoving, near the rocks, watching golden and green and dark-red weed drifting in the current. I touched a finger gently to red anemones and a starfish and tugged experimentally at blue mussel shells.

I swam farther out than I'd been before and trod water, staring back at the cove, enjoying seeing it from another angle. Near the water's edge, the Windsurfer was folded into its crumpled sail, like a broken butterfly. Behind me, *Fetha* cast a white, shimmering reflection.

Even in the suit, I was getting cold. Below me in the aqua depths, my toes felt far away and my legs were numb. My fingers, when I spread them, were white. I struck out for the sailing boat. Someone had left the ladder down at the stern; my feet groped up its rungs and I hauled myself onto *Fetha*'s swim steps. The boat rocked under me. I wiped water from my face and moved to the top step. After a few minutes, I stopped shivering.

On either side of the steps, large lockers were held shut with steel and black rubber clasps. Idly, I opened a locker and peered inside. It was bigger than I'd anticipated: several feet in both length and depth. A sail lay in the bottom, a few coils of rope, nothing interesting. I fastened the clasps back down and climbed into the cockpit. The helm was hot to the touch. I lay on the curved cockpit seat but the fiberglass was uncomfortable beneath my shoulders. I slid the hatch open — it was unlocked — and carefully climbed down the companionway steps into the cabin.

I stood in front of the little stove and imagined cooking on it. Glancing idly at the charts lying on the table, I ran my hand over the smooth teak wood of the counter. Water rocked the boat gently; it was like being in a cradle. Water lapped and chuckled against the hull. I yawned. Sleepiness poured over me in waves. The cabin was very warm.

When I poked my head out, the cove was empty. Nicholas wasn't home yet. I considered diving from the swim steps, straight down into cold water, swimming to shore. But I was too drowsy, too lazy. Also, in the suit, too hot. I peeled it off, then wandered to the berth in the bow of the boat and closed the door behind me, dropping the suit on the floor. The tiny bedroom was like a doll's house room, like a room a kid would build in a fort — a place of perfect safety. The mattress was covered with a plaid patterned fabric, blue and green. I opened a locker and pulled out a pillow and lay down. I'd have a short nap, I thought, and then I'd dive from the swim steps and meet Nicholas in the cove. I stretched like a cat, luxuriously, and closed my eyes with a smile.

CHAPTER SIXTEEN

D arkness. I peered into it, disoriented. Where was I?
The tent . . . the guestroom at Rose Mullion? No,
neither of those places. Something was wrong. Alarm
shot through me.

Where was I?

I reached out an arm and touched the smooth wood
close to my head. The bed moved beneath me, pitching
rhythmically. The boat? I thought. I was in the boat? But
I'd just fallen asleep . . . it should have been afternoon
still . . . I was only taking a nap!

I sat up in panic, pushing aside the pillow, struggling to
focus my eyes. I knuckled them hard, swallowed, took a

deep breath. There had to be a reasonable explanation. My eyes adjusted to the darkness and I knew, without doubt, that I was in the forward berth in *Fetha*. I had no idea what time it might be. I would have to swim back to the beach in the dark. Skye must be wondering where I was . . .

I pressed my face to the porthole. No cove. No cliffs, no roof line of Rose Mullion. Nothing but black heaving water. Heaving, I thought. But in the cove it had been calm, not wavy like this.

I threw myself across the bunk and pressed my face to the other porthole, fighting down panic. There was another boat out there in the dark, a boat without any lights showing on it: no white mast light, no red port and green starboard running lights. It looked like a fishing trawler, like the ones I'd seen in Falmouth harbor. On its deck, a small glow of light wavered and disappeared. A flashlight's beam, I thought. I didn't notice the smaller boat until it passed right in front of me, its motor purring softly. It was a dinghy, painted some dark color. There were three people seated in it, dark bulky shapes.

I jerked away from the glass and lay down flat. *Fetha* rocked and swung; the dinghy bumped along her toward the stern. Male voices spoke, an exclamation and then Richard's voice. I strained to hear what was being said but I couldn't discern words. Then I caught *Sacre bleu, non, non, mais aujourd'hui, nous allons, eh bien, mes amis.* They were speaking French. The bumping continued at *Fetha*'s stern.

What was happening? I felt as though I'd stumbled into a dream I couldn't wake up from, a nightmare. I curled my toes anxiously on the dark mattress.

An engine revved; I peeked through the porthole in time to see the dinghy heading back to the fishing trawler. There was only one man in it now, sitting in the stern, steering with the outboard. The dinghy disappeared against the trawler's dark bulk, and then *Fetha*'s engines kicked into life and settled into a heavy, throbbing tempo. She began swinging away from the trawler and all I could see was black heaving water again. Above in the cockpit, Richard started whistling.

I moved by instinct, sliding off the bed in silence, opening the locker door, stepping inside the small black space. I crouched down on another pillow that was stored there. Before pulling the door shut, I reached out for the wet suit and yanked it in beside me. I didn't latch the door, but held it closed with my fingers so it wouldn't swing and make a noise. Crouched there with the boat pitching under me, my mind whirled.

We're far out, I thought. There's no wind. It's a calm night with stars. The water isn't rough, but it's the way water is far out from land: a heavy, long, rolling swell. We're at sea.

Richard often sails in the Channel, I thought. I'm safe with him. He can sail in the dark. But what was he doing out here, near a vessel with no lights? Who were the men who came on board? Where were they now? No matter how hard I listened, I could hear nothing, no voices. Why were the other men silent? Where were we all going?

I had to keep fighting down waves of fear, a queasy lift and fall in my stomach. Every time my stomach rose into my throat, I swallowed hard and pressed my mouth shut. I couldn't be sick, not now, not here. I tried not to notice the smells in the locker of life jackets and wood and diesel.

Should I go on deck, greet Richard with a laugh, make a joke about being a stowaway? How could I have slept so long, so deeply? But then, I thought, it had been an eventful weekend, what with camping and swimming and playing cards late last night. I remembered how sleepy I'd been when I stretched out on the birth in *Fetha*. Now, it seemed like a lifetime ago.

My stomach rumbled. I'd missed supper. My legs cramped and I rearranged them. My fingers were tired, gripping the bottom edge of the locker door. What would I say if Richard came in here? How could I explain myself? It would be better if I was still on the bed, pretending to be asleep.

But I didn't climb out of the locker. It was as if my body knew something about the situation that I did not.

I remembered my last position of discomfort: beneath the rhododendron trees with Nicholas, spying on Peter and that strange woman and the other two men. They must have arrived by boat, Nicholas had said. Across the channel. Someone brought them in . . .

Understanding jolted through me; my muscles clenched. Oh, how could I have been so blind, so trusting, so stupid?

It was Richard all along, Richard who was smuggling, who was sailing in the Channel, meeting unlit French trawlers, taking on board illegal immigrants, ferrying them back to Rose Mullion's secret cove, sending them upcountry in his truck with Peter at the wheel.

And here I was, a witness to it all. To a criminal activity.

You don't know what my dad's like to live with, Nicholas had said by our fire at the cove. You think he's so great, but you don't know anything.

Was Richard a nationalist like Peter? I wondered. Or did he just do this for the money, the secret wads of rolled banknotes that were later spent on sports cars and equipment for his boat?

Nationalists are fanatics, my history teacher's voice said in my head. *And fanatics are always dangerous to someone.*

My stomach knotted and churned with fear. *Will you please not go on strangers' boats?* Noah had e-mailed me, and I'd gone and done just that. I thought I knew Richard but suddenly I understood: all I knew of Richard was his flashy lifestyle and the way he dressed — those superficial things that hid a stranger.

The smell of diesel seemed to fill my head until I couldn't think about anything else. I'd been in the locker all my life, cramped, nauseous, waiting to find out what would happen.

Was this how the immigrants were feeling? Were they folded up small in those empty stern storage lockers of *Fetha*'s, by the swim steps? Were they bruised and frightened, seasick? What had their lives been like at home, that they would be desperate enough to travel so far into the unknown? I wondered where these people had come from. Perhaps they came from Romania, a country gripped by poverty, or perhaps from Kosovo, a place destroyed by ethnic fighting. I recalled the newspaper article Nicholas had shown me about the woman begging in the streets of London.

The news was full of stories about illegals dying en route, frozen in the backs of trucks, trapped under trains. If this boat sinks, I thought, they'll drown in the storage compartments. And I'll drown, too. Claustrophobia engulfed me. I wanted to fling the locker door open and burst into the cockpit, gulping fresh air into my lungs. How quickly did a boat sink if a wave swamped it? It's not stormy, I scolded myself. This boat isn't going to the bottom.

I must have dozed, my body rocking to the boat's motion. I came to with a jerk as my nose bumped against my knees. I rearranged my legs, swallowed hard, listened. Overhead, a sail flapped and luffed. The jib must have been up. Maybe the wind was filling it, helping the engine to sail us home. If we were heading home. The one time that Richard had taken us sailing, I'd asked him how one man could sail a boat this size alone. He'd proudly shown me the self-furling jib, the electric winches, the auto helm pilot. "All these toys make it easy," he'd said with a laugh.

I dozed some more. This time, heavy steps awoke me. Richard, or one of the other men? Someone was in the cabin. I held my breath. A cup clattered, a tap ran. Charts or something else rustled, then the steps receded up the steps into the cockpit again. I relaxed by inches.

Night dragged on. I dozed again. The harsh rattle of the anchor chain running out brought me fully awake. I peeked through a crack in the locker door. It was still dark, before dawn. Footsteps clumped around on deck. Blurred, indistinct voices came to me. *Fetha* was barely rolling now, afloat in calmer inshore water. There was a scraping noise. The sound of storage compartments being closed. The zodiac engine purring into life. Moving away. Silence.

I crouched in the silence forever, listening to my breathing. Were we at Rose Mullion or in some foreign port? Had Richard taken the other men ashore? I needed to get ashore, too, while it was still dark, but I didn't want to run into Richard and the immigrants. There was only one path out of the cove, and I'd be following in their footsteps. Maybe Richard had taken them into the house, or maybe they'd already left with Peter in the truck. I had no way of knowing.

If I stayed here too long, Richard would find me onboard if he came back down to the boat. I climbed from the locker, so stiff I couldn't stand up. Gradually, blood flowed back into my muscles. I hauled on the wet suit, inched up the companionway steps, and lifted my eyes over the top. Around me stretched the familiar rocky headlands. *Fetha* had brought me home.

After I'd scanned the dark cove and cliff, and seen no movement, I climbed out and slipped off the back of the boat into the black water. It was scary, swimming in the night. I tried not to think of what might be swimming in the darkness below me, or around me: the trailing weed that might wrap my ankle, the unknown fish. In the cove, I crept over the shingle to the boathouse and changed back into my shorts and a T-shirt, hanging the wet suit up to dry. Then I scaled the cliff path, holding my breath when gravel grated underfoot, pausing to listen. A pale streak was spreading in the eastern sky, and the bushes in the garden were dark masses of foliage silhouetted against it. I could see my hands and legs, pale in the dim light. Ahead, the rooftop of Rose Mullion was a hard line against the horizon. I was almost to the house.

"Who's there?" barked a voice beyond the next terrace of bushes. Peter's voice.

I froze. My throat closed.

"What?" called Richard, sounding farther away.

I began to walk backward, one step at a time, the way you move away from a wild animal. Branches poked into my back. I crouched down and huddled under them.

"Thought I 'eard something," grumbled Peter.

"Probably that badger," said Richard.

A series of indistinct sounds reached my ears: gravel crunching, voices, a bump. Still crouching, I began to move back toward the cliff path. I'd wait below, in the cove, until the men had left.

"Peter!" Richard's voice called on a hushed note.

"'Ang on a minute," Peter's voice said, so close by that I swallowed a squeal of fright.

He's right there, I thought. *On the other side of the bush.*

Twigs crackled underfoot as Peter moved, shifting his weight. From farther away came the sound of fabric brushing against foliage.

"What's going on?" asked Richard, sounding closer.

"Ef tez that badger, I want a geek at en," growled Peter. "Ef tez someone gawking around, e'll wish e'd never been born."

Hair stood up on my neck. Fear ran cold down my legs. My heart jumped and galloped. I fumbled over the ground. My fingers grasped a dead stick and I flung it sideways; it cartwheeled through the darkness and fell yards away with a rustling crash.

Peter let out a harsh exclamation. "Ear that, did ee?" he hissed, his footsteps moving away toward where my stick had landed.

"Coming," said Richard.

As they moved away, I slipped off my shoes and rushed silently across a patch of dewy lawn, leaped two feet down off a terrace, and sped toward the cliff path. Panic raced blindly through me. Adrenaline lent speed to my feet; fearlessly, they carried me down the cliff path, through the smugglers' rock cut. My right big toe smashed into a rock but I ignored the stab of pain. I lowered myself off the cut carefully, trying not to dislodge the pebbles on the beach below. My heart beat so loudly I couldn't hear anything, didn't know if I was being followed.

Suddenly, voices sounded above me. The men must have been at the top of the path. Would they come down it? Stones rattled. I sprang away, racing across the beach, keeping to the hard sand, being silent. Ahead of me the boathouse yawned darkly. Should I hide inside? But it was the first place anyone would look. I stared around wildly, trapped in the cove. They would come down the path behind me, find me crouched behind a rock or in the boathouse, drag me upright by my arms.

Should I scramble over the rocks into Poldhu Cove? An image flashed through my mind of Nicholas trapped by the deep zawn, boiling with golden weed and black water.

Then, in the dim light, I saw the Windsurfer beneath

its crumpled sail, still lying at the water's edge where it had been yesterday. Without pausing to think, I folded the sail on top of it, pushed it into the water, and felt it become buoyant. I lay on it, using my hands to paddle it out past *Fetha*'s ghostly hull. Every moment, I expected to be stopped by a shout of alarm. But perhaps it was still dark enough that no one would see me against the water. Perhaps they hadn't yet traced me to the cove.

I brought the board alongside *Fetha*'s hull, bumping gently. Drifting, hidden by the hull, I listened. Would they notice that the Windsurfer was missing from the beach? Faint sounds came to me: a shout, Peter's voice, a whistle. Cautiously, I nosed the board forward to *Fetha*'s bow and peered around it into the cove. At first I didn't see anything; then, very dimly, I sensed as much as saw Peter and Blondie crossing the beach. They paused on the far side, came back, then disappeared into the boathouse. After a moment, they reappeared and headed back up the cliff path to the garden.

I lay on the board for a long time, trying to decide what to do. I knew that if Richard came down and paddled the zodiac out to *Fetha*, I'd be found. But I couldn't climb back up the path to the house; just the thought of doing so set my heart racing.

I'd sail around the headland out of sight, I decided, and make for the nameless cove where Nicholas and I'd had a fire. Then I'd climb the path to the tents, and find Nicholas there. I hoped he had slept out last night.

Feeling exposed, I paddled the board to the mouth of the cove, still trying to keep the bulk of *Fetha*'s hull between me and anyone who might be watching. At the mouth of the cove, I tried to think. What had Nicholas taught me? How did this thing work? Could I do it? I tried to focus past the sound of my heart racing, past the panic coursing through me. Think, I told my brain. *Think*.

Balance, I thought, be careful. I felt the puffs of breeze on my cheek, angled the board so the wind came from over my right shoulder, and rose carefully to my feet with the sail boom grasped in my hands. It was almost too heavy for me. Every fiber in my body strained to keep balanced on the rocking board, to pull the sail upright. A puff of wind filled it; the board began to move, cutting through the gentle swell in silence. A long breath escaped from me. I rounded the first headland and knew I was safe now: no one from Rose Mullion could see me. I began to cut across Poldhu Cove.

Dawn arrived. The black water broke into gleaming tongues of primrose yellow light. The cliffs loomed stark and huge. A banner of cloud caught the rays of the sun and burst into brilliance, while early seagulls winged over my head. As the light grew, the wind became fitful. My sail luffed and drooped, then bellied out again. I wobbled on the board. The sail tugged, drooped. I over-balanced and flew face forward into the cold water. It broke over me like pure shock and I rose to the surface gasping, hair and water in my eyes. With difficulty, I pulled myself back onto the board and lay stomach down, my clothes clinging to my body.

Gentle swells rolled under me, nudging the board along. The wind had died. I'd have to paddle. I unstepped the mast, pulled the sail onto the board, and folded it in layers. Then I lay on them and hung my arms over the sides of the board and began to paddle with both hands. The first sunlight reached me. Each swell was crested with glittering sequins of light, rolling in to hush against the jumbled rocks at the base of the cliffs.

Suddenly, a sleek head broke the surface of the water. The adult seal stared at me, its round eyes huge and limpid, like a dog's. Effortlessly, it bobbed along beside me. I stopped paddling and just drifted, watching it with delight. Its dogginess comforted me. Its whiskers were bunches of fine steel wire; the slits of its nostrils opened and closed. I called to it, and it ducked as though to submerge, but curiosity got the better of it and it remained, watching me. Did we watch each other for five minutes . . . ten?

Finally the seal sucked in air, closed its nostrils, and submerged. The water swirled where it had dived. I waited for it to reappear. I swiveled my head, waiting — then noticed what had happened. My board had drifted farther out from the cliffs, from Poldhu Cove. I was facing almost into the open channel. The swell was larger now, rolling me rhythmically.

Choppily, hurrying, I paddled with my arms, swinging the nose of the board back toward the next headland. All I had to do was get around it and I'd be safe, and Nicholas might be lying in his tent at the top of the path. I settled down to some steady paddling. The sun was warm now, burning off the slight blue heat haze. My stubbed toe stung in the salt water that sloshed over the board occasionally.

My arms began to ache. I stopped to rest and looked

around. *I was farther out*. Was I farther out? Where exactly had I been before I stopped to look at the seal? Had the cliffs been closer or did I just imagine they'd been closer?

I fought down panic and began to paddle, hard. I gritted my teeth and kept on even though my arms were aching, burning, every muscles hurting. Ten minutes, I thought, I'll paddle for ten minutes before I check my position again. But how would I know what ten minutes felt like, out here in a place where I'd never expected to be, where I was all alone, where there were no safety lines, nothing but blue water and pain?

CHAPTER SEVENTEEN

Finally, I stopped and looked around. I *was* farther out. Was it a current, a strong, deep current, invisible, holding me, pulling me out to sea? Or was it a riptide that would suck me under, slurping me into its long mouth of darkness? Or was the tide itself dropping, ebbing away from the coves and the cliffs, taking me with it for six hours?

I'll slide into the water, I thought, and kick the board along. Legs are stronger than arms. And my legs weren't tired the way my arms were. I sat up, the board rocking. That's when I saw them.

The three jellyfish seemed to move without effort, as

though dragged along on invisible strings. They were pale purple-white, semitranslucent, like clouds. Their sails drifted above the water . . . and underneath them, I knew, trailed long tentacles, like whips, that could wrap around me and poison me, lacerating my skin with stinging barbs and releasing toxins into my nervous system. Skye had warned me about them: the Man-o-war. In horrified fascination I stared at them as they drifted past, fifteen feet away, silent, deadly, beautiful in the sunlight.

There were others, I noticed, farther away. They were like a ghostly armada. I remembered Skye warning me that they traveled in large groups, formed colonies in which individual members played different roles.

Long after they'd floated on, I sat and stared into the waves. Then I lay down on the board again. I pressed my eyes shut and thought about Skye coming home last night to an empty apartment. Would she be worried about me or would she just start painting the next piece of canvas with renewed inspiration, disappearing off into her own world with no concern for my whereabouts? No, I couldn't believe that. Surely by now she'd be looking for me.

And what about Nicholas? Was he asleep in his tent, with Blondie lolling at his side? If I thought about him really, really hard, would some disturbance in the airwaves awaken him and make him glance out to sea, where he might spot me drifting by? But perhaps he was at Rose Mullion, safe and fast asleep in his room, a world away from me.

I would not think about the deep dark water beneath me, how cold it was, how quickly it would numb me and chill me, stealing away my strength, my life.

I wouldn't think about its strong invisible currents that had me in their grip, that were pulling me farther away from the rocky coastline, from the hot smell of furze and flowers, from the stillness of solid ground. I wouldn't think about the jellyfish, their thirty-feet-long pale tentacles trailing through the water, their silent approach, their deadly stings.

If I thought about these things I would fly into pieces, give into a storm of hot tears, of white blinding panic. Instead, I thought about the sun warming my shoulder blades, the rustle of the sail when I moved an arm, the hard tilt of the board under my hipbones. I thought about my breathing, how it flowed in and out of my lungs, lifting my ribs, one breath after another . . . after another . . . another. I felt the edges of my teeth, lined up, gritting together.

In a little while, once I'd fought down my panic, I would think of a plan to save myself, but I couldn't do it yet. So I thought about Noah, how much I wanted to be with him wherever he was, how his freckles looked, the exact color of his hair. Soon, in another four days, we'd be flying home and Noah and I would be together again. Please. Oh, please. I suddenly couldn't bear the thought that I might never return home, that Noah would be without his twin. *You're out of your depth in salt water, it's deep stuff*, he had told me. Noah, I answered now in my head, you are oh, so right. Noah, help! Tell me what to do! Gradually, as I focused on his face, my heartbeat steadied and my panic receded. *Think about it*, his voice spoke, in the tone he always used when he wanted me to follow his logic, his practical work-it-out, use-your-brain logic.

My mind was so far away with Noah that, at first, it paid no attention to what my ears were telling it. Then it began to listen to the sound of a motor. Who was coming? Had the men seen me after all and come chasing after me? Which would be worse: facing them or drifting along alone? Or did the sound belong to a fisherman's boat, as he motored out to check crab traps?

"Stella!"

Carefully, I opened my eyes and, handling my body like something impossibly fragile and precious, I slowly sat up. Nicholas' dark hair and lean face were visible over the bow of the zodiac as it bounced toward me, throwing a wave of white spray.

I didn't speak or move. I sat on my board like someone who'd survived a shipwreck, who'd been alone so long that all words were forgotten. I licked my dry lips, tried to swallow. Nicholas throttled back and brought the gray rubber pontoons alongside. After shifting into neutral, he reached out his long, tough arms and hauled me onboard. He hauled the Windsurfer and sail onboard, too. Then he sat in the bottom of the boat and put both his arms around me. He pressed his face against my cheek and held it there, hard and warm.

The engine sputtered in idle. Blue diesel smoke drifted away into the salty air. The sea flexed itself under the rubber hull, lifted it beneath us with easy power. Light glittered in my eyes; the dark hair on Nicholas' arms swam in and out of focus. I could feel the tendons in his arms, strained tight.

"Stella, I thought you'd drowned," he said finally, the words choking him.

"I thought I was going to drown, too," I croaked.

He kissed my cheek, my ear, my eyelid. His breath was warm in my hair.

"Oh Stella," he said. "You're my best friend. What happened to you? Where have you been?"

I sat up and turned to look at him. What could I tell him? Where should I begin? "It's your dad," I blurted out. "He's the smuggler, Nicholas. I went to sea last night on *Fetha* with him, by mistake."

"What?" Nicholas' eyes stretched wide. Then he glanced over my shoulder at the receding cliffs and kneeled by the outboard, shifting it into gear. "Wait. The tide's dropping," he said. "Tell me when we get to shore."

"Don't go home!" I said, a last spasm of panic in my throat. "Go to the cove below the tents."

I watched the wake unwind behind us on the swells. Soon we were in the cove, then the zodiac beached itself on the sand with a jerk and Nicholas jumped out, grabbing the painter, waves breaking around his knees. He tied the painter around a boulder and we sat on the beach while I told him what had happened. As I talked, Nicholas' face turned to stone.

He slammed a fist into a palm and glared at his hands. "It's for the money," he said angrily. "He'd do anything for the money. Greedy bugger. He'll get caught one of these days or maybe I'll turn him in first. Teach him a lesson. That would serve him right."

I waited while Nicholas fumed, clenching and unclenching his fists, whitening his knuckles.

"And Peter! I should have taken all that nationalistic

stuff seriously. I thought he was just one of those blokes who likes to mouth off about the English while hoisting a pint. But he's for real."

"What do you mean?"

"He's a nationalist. Like, the Cornish have always smuggled for two reasons. One, for the income. Two, for the sheer bloody-mindedness of doing whatever they wanted contrary to English laws. To sort of prove they didn't have to be bossed around by the English."

"Oh." I watched while Nicholas ground a heel into the granular sand, creating a miniature landscape of ridges and valleys. Finally, I laid a tentative hand on his sleeve.

"I have to get to Falmouth," I said. "Skye's going to kill me."

"She's not home yet," Nicholas said. "She rang about five-thirty yesterday when I got home from the dentist to say there's a change in plans and that she's not coming home until tomorrow. Wednesday."

"Oh." The cool, sinking feeling in my stomach took me by surprise. I hadn't known I wanted to hear the sound of Skye's voice so much, wanted to walk into the flat in Falmouth and pour my story out to her. But she wouldn't be home until the day after tomorrow.

"I rang you twice last evening, in Falmouth, to give you Skye's message," Nicholas continued. "I thought you'd be there. But you didn't answer. So I left a message on your answering service but you never called back. I rang again early this morning to make sure that you were there, that you'd got the message. I figured it was weird you hadn't called back. You still weren't answering your phone this morning. That's when I started getting worried about you. I checked the guest room at Rose Mullion, then I went down to the cove and found the Windsurfer missing. I came out in the zodiac in case you'd taken the Windsurfer and got into difficulties."

"Did you see your dad this morning?"

"Nope. But I saw the lorry and the car going up the lane when I walked in from the tent."

"What am I going to do?" I asked blankly. "I can't go back to Rose Mullion, Nicholas. I just can't."

"Hey, it's alright," he said. "You're safe now. Climb the path up the cliffs here, then take the track east until you come to the first stile. Then you'll be in the lane for Nancherrow, a farm. Take the lane out through the farmyard to the road. Wait for me there. I'm going to take the zodiac home and grab our stuff from the house. We'll go into Falmouth together on the bus."

"What will you tell your dad?"

"That he's going to jail. Oh, don't look so worried. He's probably still out anyway. But if he's there, I'll say the Windsurfer drifted away and I had to go and get it with the zodiac. Can you remember how to find the road?"

"Stile, Nancherrow lane, road," I said.

I hugged myself, watching Nicholas push the zodiac into the water, coil the painter, lower the outboard propeller. "Be careful," I called and he flashed me a smile and waved. I waited until the zodiac was just a dot on the bright water, rounding the headland, its engine note dying in my ears. I was alone again. I wanted to lie on the warm sand, feel the solid bulk of the world beneath me, plaster myself against it, and never let go again. But

I didn't. I turned my back on the sea and scrambled up the hot, dusty path between clumps of thrift and sea poppy. At the top, I paused to rest, feeling lightheaded. I should have asked Nicholas to bring food.

In Nancherrow's fields, the barley heads were heavy and golden. Overhead, a kestrel hovered, holding the sky on its back. I shaded my eyes and looked out to sea, trying to imagine myself floating along, far out, where heat haze blended sea and sky together in one color. A place where anything could happen. Where my body, so warm and strong, so real, might vanish and leave no trace of itself.

At that moment, I knew it was not the shape of a body that mattered most, nor what clothes one draped it in. What was important was simply a body's existence, its beautiful state of being alive.

When I reached the road, I waited nervously. Every approaching car found me poised for flight, but where would I run if Peter or Richard found me standing here? Had either of them seen me well enough to recognize me in the dim dawn light? Had I left anything on *Fetha* that would betray my presence there?

Finally, exhaustion set in and I slumped against a gate post, thirsty and hot. My head ached. My ears sang. When the bus finally arrived I almost didn't notice Nicholas' face pressed anxiously to the glass next to the back seat. I climbed onboard, fumbled in my pockets for my change, then pawed stupidly through it, peering at the weird British coins. I felt as if I'd been away from money for a long time. Finally, Nicholas strode forward and paid my fare.

In Falmouth, we headed straight for the apartment; I kept glancing over my shoulder as though at any moment Peter or Richard would materialize from the crowd, would reach out and grab me from behind. The apartment felt strange without Skye. Her easel was empty, her brushes packed away, her paint rags cleared up. I wasn't going to admit that I missed all the clutter, but the apartment did seem different without it, less friendly.

I paced through the rooms, convincing myself they were empty. What was the matter with me? I had thought I'd feel safe once I got here, but I didn't feel safe. Without Skye, the apartment seemed impersonal, like hotel accommodation.

"This is the first place your dad will look for me," I told Nicholas, who was peering into the fridge. "And Peter knows how to find me, too. I can't stay here on my own."

"Just let Dad or Peter turn up here and I'll ring the police," Nicholas muttered angrily. "I'll turn them in. You could have drowned out there!"

"How come Skye's delayed?" I asked.

"She said that tonight there's an opening for a show, and she's hoping to meet some other artists who'll attend it. She asked if you were alright and I said you were fine. I didn't know you were out on *Fetha*."

"I can't stay here," I repeated anxiously. "Where can I go?"

Nicholas prowled restlessly around the room, taking savage bites from one of the apples he'd found in the vegetable tray. Each time he passed the telephone he scowled as though he'd like to lift the receiver and call the police right then and there.

I gnawed at my own apple and tried to figure out where I could go. My thoughts felt scattered, like spilled beads. If only I had friends here, people like Ashley and her mom who knew me well and would open their door wide when I appeared on the step! Or if only I had family here who knew me! Then it dawned on me there was someone in Cornwall who knew me, who wanted to see me.

"Do you know Lavinia Trebilcock?" I asked.

"She's a cousin of my mother's."

"I have her phone number; I'll call and see if I can stay with her," I said.

"Ask her if I can come too."

"You're not going back to your dad's," I said, and it wasn't really a question.

"No," Nicholas replied, the word shooting out of his mouth with the speed and density of a bullet. I didn't ask him anything else, just started leafing through my stuff for Lavinia's number, written in my father's strong hand.

An elderly voice answered the phone, not one of those whispery, faint old voices but the kind of voice that holds a spark and a twinkle.

"Eh, me dear maid, you do sound just like yer mother," Lavinia told me with delight. "You and Nicholas come along then; I'll look for you around teatime. You do need to change trains in Liskeard for Looe. I'm down beside the harbor; the cottage is called Nankilly. Oh, tez a fair treat to hear yer voice."

I was smiling when I hung up the phone. "We can go," I told Nicholas. "I just need to grab some stuff first."

In my room, I crammed things into my backpack. A kind of feverish haste gripped me. My hands fumbled through clean underwear and over coat hangers. I packed Maggie's journal, my poems, my mother's picture, my flute, two favorite dresses, a sweater. I didn't really know what I needed, when I'd be back, what I was planning. I just wanted to be somewhere else where I could feel safe. This was how refugees packed, running from a threat, not knowing what would be needed at the next place.

I slung my pack over my shoulder and joined Nicholas in the kitchen. "You ready?" I asked.

"Almost." He was cutting up pieces of cardboard snitched from Skye's supply. He placed a piece on each side of several of his paintings to protect them, then slid them back into his pack. I hadn't noticed until now that he'd brought his pack, that it was stuffed and bulging. He straightened up and lifted his jacket from the floor. I watched him fumble through its pockets and pull out the crumpled packet of Woodbine cigarettes. He dropped it into the garbage under the sink and gave me a lopsided grin.

"Whatcher staring at, wench? Let's move out," he said. "Bring your clobber."

When we arrived at Falmouth station, I sat on a bench with our bags but Nicholas paced restlessly up and down the platform as if his thoughts were nipping his heels. Then he went into the pay telephone kiosk and I saw him riffling through the pages of the telephone directory. Twice he lifted the receiver but each time hung it back into its cradle. Finally, with a disgruntled kick at the door, he emerged. "I'll wait until we're farther away," he muttered as he walked past me. "I'll call the police from Lavinia's."

I nodded and bent back over the train schedule in my hand. It looked as though we'd need a train to Truro, one to Liskeard, a third to Looe. "I think we have a problem," I said. "How much is this going to cost?"

A blank look came over Nicholas' face. He fumbled through his pockets again, peered into his wallet, dug through his pack. By now, I was doing the same. Between us, we had three pounds.

"We can't go anywhere with only three pounds," I wailed. "Do you have more money at Rose Mullion?"

Nicholas shook his head. Gloomily, he wandered to the end of the concrete platform and back, kicking an empty Tango can.

"Is there money in your flat?" he asked.

"I wouldn't think so." I glanced at my watch; we had twenty minutes before the train arrived. I was feeling even more like a refugee, someone with no place of safety, no doors opening, no connections to family or friends. Miserably, I wished Skye was around with her common-sense approach.

"I'm going to call Skye," I decided, gesturing at the pay phone inside its red box. "She left me her number in London. Maybe she can help. I don't have much change, do you have any?"

"Not much." Nicholas handed me a 50 pence coin and a 10 pence coin. "You'll have to talk fast," he warned.

I dialed, clutching the receiver tightly. Please, please be there, I prayed as the telephone gave its strange buzzing ring.

"Hello?"

I pushed the coins into the pay phone's slot, heard them rattle to the bottom.

"Skye! It's Stella. Oh, you're there, I thought —"

"You just caught me. I'm heading out the door to a workshop," she said. "I'm having a great time here. Are you okay? Did you get my message from Nicholas?"

"Yes, I did. Skye —"

"Sorry, Stella. Hold on."

I waited impatiently, listening to faint background voices, Skye telling someone that she'd catch them up, the sound of a door closing. The telephone began beeping a warning in my ear and I struggled to feed my last coin into its slot. I couldn't believe how much a phone call cost in Britain.

"Sorry about that," Skye said in my ear. "The rest of my group are going out."

"Skye, I need some money," I said urgently. "Is there any in the apartment?"

"Yes," she said without hesitation. "In my room, in the closet, there's a patchwork bag. Inside the bag, there's a change purse with some money in it. How much do you need? Is everything alright?"

"I just need some for —" I started to say, but the telephone began beeping again, asking for more money. "I'll call you back later today," I said. "I'm going to —"

The telephone ran out of money and cut me off.

"Any luck?" Nicholas asked.

"There's money in the apartment," I said. "We'll have to go back and fetch it, then catch a later train."

Hurriedly, we set off with our heavy packs.

I could hardly bear the delay; the feeling that I shouldn't be out walking around in broad daylight, that at any moment the silver car or the white van would stop beside me, that an arm would reach out for me.

"Blimey, you walk fast," Nicholas complained.

"I just want to get away."

CHAPTER EIGHTEEN

"Did you know my mother well?" I asked Lavinia, when I'd swallowed the last bite of the delicious pasties she'd made for lunch.

"Oh es, me dear," Lavinia replied, with a smile that crinkled her small face up like a withered apple. The overhead light glinted on her glasses and behind them I knew her eyes were sparkling. There was something about her that reminded me of my great-grandmother Maggie, something resilient and strong.

"Es," she repeated. "Yer mother came 'ere when she was a girl, with her own mother. Then she came alone when she was quite a young woman, seventeen maybe.

The last time she stayed 'ere weth me was the summer before she was married to yer dear father."

I watched Lavinia pour tea, her thin hands like claws around the handle. "What was she like?" I asked.

Lavinia cut thick slices off a homemade fruitcake and pushed one across to me before she answered. "Like?" she repeated at last. "She were like a bright flame, quick and beautiful. Mind, she weren't just a 'andsome face. She were right smart too, sharp as a tack. Did well for herself. There were a lot more to her than a pretty face. She 'ad a sweet heart, a kind tongue."

We ate our cake in silence, while Lavinia's cup of tea steamed. "Oh es, she were beautiful in her heart," said Lavinia. "And she adored you."

"Me?" I asked. My voice came out in a squeak.

"Thought the sun rose and set with you, her dear little maid," Lavinia said. "Many's the time she's written me a letter and talked of nothing but you. Course, yer father and yer brother were in there too. She loved you all."

"She wrote to you?" I asked in surprise.

"Es, from time to time. Christmas mainly. Course, she were always busy with her work and her family. But toward the end, she wrote almost every week."

I pressed my finger onto my plate, mushing up cake crumbs. I was afraid to ask the next question. It was too big. It was stuck in my throat. I stared over Lavinia's shoulder and through the tiny cottage window toward the harbor. Nicholas was out there, walking around and thinking about his father. Trying to decide what to do.

"Ave another slice of cake, me dear," Lavinia urged,

but I shook my head and screwed up my courage. "What did my mother say at the end?" I asked.

"Can't zackly recall all of it," Lavinia said kindly. "Tez some years ago now. Awful worried about you though, she was. Wrote to me from the hospital, wondering how you'd manage without her. Said you were her star."

"I don't know what she meant," I said anxiously.

"Meant? Why, just that she loved you. Loved yer red curls and yer saucy grin. Loved the pictures you made her in school and brought to the hospital. Said you were a real tomboy, always dirty as a tinker. Said you were bright as a spark. She hoped you'd —"

"What?" I asked.

"Can't remember zackly how she put it. Hoped you'd follow yer own talents. That was it. Follow yer own talents. Said you could sing like a skylark, Stella. Course, that's the Cornish in you. We can all sing. Said you were always printing little stories too. You doing any writing?"

"Yes," I said, my voice steady and strong. "I might be a writer."

"You put yer mind to it, you'll do it," Lavinia said confidently. "You'm just like yer mother, her very image. She could do anything she put 'er mind to. I think she 'ad some regrets, though, at the end."

"Regrets?" I asked. I waited anxiously for Lavinia's answer while a seagull cried outside and sunlight slid across Lavinia's starched white tablecloth, her china cups and plates, the rough white walls of her cottage.

Lavinia sighed. "P'raps regret is too strong a word for it," she said. "What yer mother felt at the end was she'd spent too much time worrying about superficial stuff, clothes and fashion. It weren't all glamour, you know. She 'ad some hard times, struggled with her health."

"What do you mean?"

"Eating disorders, isn't that what they call them? Trying so 'ard to stay slim that you can't keep yer food down."

Lavinia's mottled hands pressed the tablecloth smooth, flattening out the slightest creases. I stared at them, breathless, struck dumb.

"Anorexia?" I asked. "My mother had anorexia?"

"She struggled with it in her teens. She were spindly as a clothes' peg. Then she was in 'ospital twice with it, when you were very young," Lavinia said. "You wouldn't remember."

"Is that what she died of?"

"No, no, t'was the breast cancer killed her. Though sometimes I wonder . . . if she'd had more flesh on 'er bones, maybe she would 'ave been stronger to fight the cancer. But that's not for us to know now."

I stared blindly at Lavinia's hands, smoothing and smoothing the tablecloth as if to smooth away the sorrow in my mother's life, the mountain ranges rearing up in my mind. "No one ever told me this," I whispered.

Lavinia laid one hand over my own. Her skin was soft and worn as chamois leather. "Yer dad's a dear man," she said. "He loved yer mother like life itself. Only way for him to get on with life, for the sake of you and Noah, was to throw himself into his work, I imagine. Yer mother told me, he wasn't one to talk about his feelings."

Pass me the screwdriver. Hand me the hammer. Just

don't ask about your mother, the story behind the laughter, the things I couldn't fix.

I pressed my hands over my ears, but it was too late for that. Lavinia had told me what I had come so far to hear.

For a long while the clock ticked. Lavinia's hands were still, folded on the cloth. Finally, she cleared her throat with an apologetic cough.

"Yer mother 'oped you'd pay attention to something else besides all that glamour," she said. "She 'oped that you'd stay strong inside. Sent me a picture once of you walking on the beam in the barn, Stella."

"Oh, Noah and I were always doing that," I said.

Lavinia laughed. "Es well, yer mother sent me the picture and she wrote on the back of it. P'raps I can find it for you, it might be around somewhere."

I wandered to the window and looked out, while Lavinia went into the room she called the parlor to search for the picture. I could hear drawers and cupboards opening and closing. I wouldn't think about the photo with my mother's message on the back, about how badly I wanted to hold it, to run my fingers over her handwriting. I tried to think about Nicholas instead. He'd been very quiet since we arrived at Lavinia's house the previous afternoon, quiet while she chatted and fed us, quiet while I phoned Skye in London, quiet as we climbed the narrow stairs to go early to bed. Now, I could see him on the harbor wall, talking to a man mending a green nylon fishing net that was spread out over the stones. What would Nicholas do about his father, who was a criminal? What would I do, now that I knew more of the truth about my mother?

"Ere tez then," said Lavinia triumphantly, coming into the kitchen with the picture held in one hand against her flowered apron. I tried not to snatch it when she held it out. I stared at the front for a long time, putting off the moment when I'd turn it over. Maybe all my mother had written on the back was a date or my name. I wanted more. I wanted a message.

In the picture, I was midway across the beam. I looked so small, so high up. How had I done that so many times without ever falling? I was wearing red denim overalls, white sneakers. Sun, slanting in through cracks in the boards, flared in my short bright hair. I was smiling.

I flipped the picture over, while Lavinia rattled cups and saucers in her shaky grasp, clearing the table. There was more than a date and a name on the back of the picture. *Stella in the barn, June 1991*, I read. And under it: *My star because she has a brave heart and can do whatever she chooses.*

I read the words over and over. It was not only for my red hair that my mother had loved me. It was not because of her dreams for my future that she called me a star. Maybe it hadn't mattered one bit to her what I chose to do, whether I sang or wrote, danced or did something ordinary like working in a grocery store. I was her star because of what was inside me, my brave heart that sent me out along the beam, balancing, smiling, sure of my feet. Maybe she would never have cared at all whether I played her flute, whether I went to modeling school. It was not for these things that she loved me.

Finally, I understood her last letter to me. *A mother's wish is that her children don't repeat her mistakes.* My mother's mistake: a love affair with glossy surfaces; windows that reflected the length of her legs; mirrors that held the tilt of her smile; magazine photographs that captured the tiny waist of this woman who designed clothes and looked as good in them as the models. My mother's mistake: telling her body what to do, not listening to its response. A kind of deafness, as if being blinded by images of beauty had closed her ears, closed down her brain cells.

"Now, dear, I'll take off this pinny and we'll go sit somewhere more comfortable," Lavinia said. I turned to see her untying her apron. The white tablecloth had been replaced by a plastic one of yellow gingham.

"Ef you want, you can keep that picture," Lavinia said. "You take it home weth you. Yer mother would want you to have it, the dear soul."

I nodded, not trusting my voice for a moment. Then I thanked her and slid the photo carefully into the front pocket of my shirt, over my heart.

"Come along then. Shall we sit in the parlor?" Lavinia asked, but Nicholas was tugging at my thoughts.

"I'm going outside for a bit," I said. "I should check on Nicholas."

Lavinia's front door opened right onto the harbor wall. I walked across the granite stones, being careful of the fishing nets. At the edge of the wall, Nicholas was sitting on a bollard, staring down into the harbor. The tide was out. Fishing boats leaned tipsily on the mud and sand, and two seagulls argued over a dead crab.

I sat down on the stones and leaned my back against the bollard. I wanted to blurt out what Lavinia had told me about my mother, but I knew this was not the right time. Maybe I'd save it for Noah, even Ashley.

"Heya. You okay?" I asked Nicholas.

"He is my dad," Nicholas said abruptly. "I mean, he's not an evil stranger or something. He makes me mad, but he's the only dad I've got, Stella. If I turn him in, he'll go to jail, right? I don't think I can do that to him."

"It doesn't seem very loyal," I agreed.

"He's not all bad," Nicholas continued, as if pleading with me to understand. "He did take us sailing and riding."

"He bought us cameras," I added.

"Those people he helps, they're from terrible places. If he didn't smuggle them, they might all be dead in their own countries."

"Yes."

I remembered how I'd felt, scrunched up in *Fetha*'s locker, alone, terrified. I thought about the BBC newscasts and the other ones, at home in Canada, about the bodies dead in trucks, the Chinese apprehended off Vancouver, the refugee camps, the people who were denied refugee status and sent back again. I wondered how it felt when there was not one single place of safety for you in the whole world.

"But I mean, he shouldn't be taking their money, right?" Nicholas asked. His voice sounded drained and flat. I leaned my shoulder against his knee.

"Do we know for sure that he is?" I asked.

"We know that Peter is, so Dad must be getting some of it, too. Something must be paying for his toys and his pricey house," Nicholas said. "He never used to be rich, even though money was the thing he cared about most. And think about when he took us places this summer."

I thought back and remembered Richard buying us cameras and pony rides, ice cream and souvenirs. He never slid a wallet from his back pocket; instead he took out a wad of bank notes and peeled money off it. The wad was thick and comprised of big bills. Richard's easy way with money had impressed me; it seemed worldly and foreign. Now, when I recalled it more soberly, I knew it wasn't normal to carry such wads of cash.

"The situation is not black and white," I said at last. "It's kind of gray. And I won't tell anyone, Nicholas. Only Skye had to know when I phoned her last night."

"He's not hurting anyone," Nicholas said. "He's just being greedy. And he's breaking the laws that are in place to keep Britain for the Brits."

"I guess countries need laws," I said. "It's like having a door that you can close on a house. If it's wide open, anyone can walk in."

"But you know what it's like in Kosovo and places at war," Nicholas argued.

I nodded. I had seen the news footage: the hopeless faces pressed to train windows, the shelled-out villages littered with bodies, the children crying in the camps. Who could blame them for leaving, for squeezing themselves small and flat, for paying their life savings to be taken away somewhere safer?

It was the money that was the problem, I thought. You didn't take money from people who had nothing left in the world, who'd lost their wives and fathers, their children, their photo albums and farms, their cows and their cars. It was like stealing their last hope. And you didn't drive them upcountry and abandon them in a dark alley, to panhandle and beg. If you were trying to help people, this was not how you did it. But I wasn't going to say this to Nicholas; he was smart enough to know it.

"What should I do?" Nicholas asked. "I know he's a criminal but he's still my dad. I can't go to the police about him. Maybe I should confront him, tell him I know what he's doing. Threaten him with what I know."

"That might be dangerous," I protested.

"But he shouldn't be allowed to keep on smuggling," Nicholas argued. "Someone has to stop him."

"Why don't you wait and talk to your mom?" I said. "She'll be here to fetch you tomorrow."

Nicholas nodded. "Guess you're right. Maybe it would be easier for her to turn him in. Maybe she could somehow do it anonymously. Give the police a tip-off and let them figure it out themselves from there."

"Yes."

In the ensuing silence, I watched him shift uncomfortably on the bollard. When I spoke his name he didn't reply, so I stood up and moved in front of him, blocking his view of the harbor. His eyes seemed gray instead of blue today, and his skin looked tight around his mouth. I tugged on his sleeve to get his attention.

"You're still going to get your name on the front of books you illustrate, right?" I said. "And you can still go home when your mom arrives to fetch you. You don't have to live with him, Nicholas. You don't even have to visit him again if you don't want to."

"No, I guess not. 'What I Did with My Summer

Holidays: Visited My Father the Criminal,'" he said bleakly.

I wished there was something I could say to make him feel better.

"Listen," I said. "This doesn't make any difference to me. You're still my really special friend. I don't feel any different about you; I know you're a good person."

"Thanks," he said quietly. After a minute, he pulled his silver Celtic ring off and held it out to me in one palm. "Will it fit you?" he asked.

"Me?" I took it in surprise, slid its intricate pattern of silver knots over one finger. Our hands were the same shape; we had the same long fingers. The ring fit me.

"Keep it," he said.

"Didn't someone special give it to you?" I asked.

"Nah, I bought it. I can get another one. I want you to have it."

"Thanks, Nicholas. Really. And you're coming to stay in Canada next summer. Promise?"

"Promise," he agreed, his eyes suddenly bluer as he smiled up at me. "You can take me canoeing and break my leg. Get your revenge for this smuggling stuff."

"Sounds cool to me," I teased and he stood up suddenly from the bollard and laughed.

"Hey, look!" he said. "She got here fast; she beat my mom."

I turned in the direction of his pointing arm. Skye was coming along the harbor wall toward us. One of her baggy, uncool dresses with green and purple swirls was flapping around her legs. It was the brightest thing in the whole village of Looe; it sang against the whitewashed granite cottages, the muddy harbor. Her worn sandals slapped on the stones and her hennaed hair made a crazy, wild halo around her head. There was a focused, intent look of concern on her face. It was directed at us.

Something warm and happy welled up in me. "Skye!" I yelled.

When she reached us, she hugged us both at once, one arm around each of us. Hugging her felt like . . . coming to a safe country. It felt like I was halfway home.

Her weird Indian perfume made me sneeze. "Yuck. What is that stuff? It should be banned," I said.

Her laughter was the best thing I'd heard all day. "Are you both in one piece?" she asked, craning her head back to look at us. "Yep, you look okay to me. You're good kids, you know that? You did the right thing to come here. I've been worried out of my mind since your call, Stella. I'm sorry you had to go through all this."

Our eyes met. I felt her concern sweep into me like a kind of current, a sea current carrying us closer together.

"Do I have to go back to Falmouth?" I asked, and she shook her head. "No, I'll go down and get our stuff. We're flying home in two days. You can stay here until we leave." She gave my arm a reassuring squeeze and right at that moment, as though the knowledge flowed out of her hand and into my arm, I realized something.

"It was your 'mad money,' wasn't it?" I said. "You gave us your mad money for the train fare."

"Yes," she replied. "I forgot to take it to London with me."

"I'll pay you back," I promised.

"It's already bought the best thing possible: your safety," she said.

I smiled at her. I mean, really smiled with my heart in it. So maybe it hadn't been a lot of money but it had been a lot to Skye. She hardly ever had money to spend on fun things; she was always scraping funds together to pay for rent, paintbrushes, food. She had given me her special money without even knowing what I needed it for. I knew then that I was forgiven for my rudeness. And I realized that maybe Skye and I had more in common than I'd thought. Being a writer was like being a painter; both created pictures, but simply used different mediums. Perhaps I would let Skye read some of my poems as long as she didn't do anything too weird on the trip home.

"Yoo hoo, tea's ready!"

We turned to see Lavinia standing in the doorway in her flowered pinny, waving at us.

"Coming!" Skye called, and she linked her arms through mine and Nicholas'. Together, we headed in for scones and raspberry jam and clotted cream.

Epilogue

The Boeing leveled off over the Irish Sea, heading west through time zones and rumpled clouds. I pressed my face to the window and stared down at the blue sea. It was the same water that surged against Cornwall's cliffs, far to the south, and that washed the white sand beaches in the Isles of Scilly. It was the same water that covered the land that lay between: Atlantis, the lost land of Lyonesse. Somewhere, far below, long ago, Trevanion had escaped on his white horse.

"This is your Captain speaking," came a voice over the sound system. "We'll be cruising today at 33,000

feet. Weather conditions are fair with scattered cloud
and we should have a pleasant flight to Toronto."

At my side, Skye opened her book, *The Zen of
Creativity*.

"Are you still reading that?" I asked. "You've been
reading it forever."

"I didn't read much in Cornwall," she said. "I was too
busy being creative."

It was strange, how long it seemed since we had flown
over this same body of water, heading east toward
London and our holiday. It seemed like we should have
had time to read all the books we'd ever wanted to in
that long stretch of time.

I settled down in my seat more comfortably and
thought about myself, flying home. I saw myself like a
girl in a movie: a girl at 33,000 feet, a tall slim girl with
a shaggy haircut growing out. Her dress was crumpled,
her suitcase a jumble of souvenirs and dirty clothes. Her
long legs were brown and scratched by blackberry vines;
one toe was stubbed and wore a bandage in her platform
sandals. A silver Celtic ring circled one finger with a
band of intricate knots, and the skin on her arms smelled
of salt. She was going to be a writer.

I smiled to myself. I knew I could do this if I chose to.
I'd had a mother who stood in the hay and clapped while
I walked the beam in the barn. She trusted my balance.
She trusted me to learn from her mistakes and now I was
learning. It didn't matter anymore what she had hoped
or planned for my future. Finally, I understood that my
mother belonged to Atlantis, a world that was gone. But

I was traveling forward into the future. I was a girl with a white horse.

Our last night in Cornwall, asleep in Lavinia's high, old-fashioned bed in a room smelling of lavender beneath the eaves, I'd dreamed my horse.

I'd dreamed a beach, a silver beach like a ribbon in the moonlight. Waves tumbled on its shore. Sand dunes rose from the beach, steep and scattered with marram grass that swayed in the wind. There were winding paths leading up the dunes. I was on a white horse, pure white without a blemish. The mare wore neither saddle nor bridle. She carried me up the dunes, through the rippling grasses in the moonlight. She didn't slip or falter. She carried me upward surely and steadily, although the soft sand ran like water under her hooves, although she sank in it to her fetlocks. Her muscles flowed beneath me. She rose through the dunes like a cloud; she could see the paths in the dark. She was mine, and I would never fall from her back. She carried me away from the restless water, from the waves on the sand, from the sea that covered Atlantis.

She was setting me free.